P9-BJQ-070

KNIGHT LIFE

The Hardys ran through the hotel, hoping to shake the man who was chasing them. "In here," Joe yelled, running through a door labeled Employees Only. Frank followed, then slammed the door and bolted it behind them.

Frank sank to one knee to catch his breath. He noticed he was kneeling in dirt instead of tile or carpet. Then he became aware of a noise like thunder—a rolling, staccato sound that seemed to be growing louder.

Frank raised his head. A horse in medieval armor was bearing down on them. Astride the horse was a knight, also in full armor.

"W-wait a minute," Frank stammered as he stood up, wondering if he'd been knocked unconscious and was dreaming. The knight's lance was pointed directly at him.

Both boys whirled to see another knight on horseback charging from the other side. "It's real!" Joe shouted.

"You bet it's real," Frank yelled. "And we're caught in the middle."

Books in THE HARDY BOYS CASEFILES™ Series

Available from ARCHWAY Paperbacks

FINAL GAMBIT

FRANKLIN W. DIXON

AN ARCHWAY PAPERBACK
Published by POCKET BOOKS
New York   London   Toronto   Sydney   Tokyo   Singapore

This book is a work of fiction. Names, characters, places and incidents are either the product of the author's imagination or are used fictitiously. Any resemblance to actual events or locales or persons, living or dead, is entirely coincidental.

AN ARCHWAY PAPERBACK *Original*

An Archway Paperback published by
POCKET BOOKS, a division of Simon & Schuster Inc.
1230 Avenue of the Americas, New York, NY 10020

Copyright © 1992 by Simon & Schuster Inc.
Produced by Mega-Books of New York, Inc.

All rights reserved, including the right to reproduce
this book or portions thereof in any form whatsoever.
For information address Pocket Books, 1230 Avenue
of the Americas, New York, NY 10020

ISBN: 0-671-73098-3

First Archway Paperback printing April 1992

10 9 8 7 6 5 4 3 2 1

THE HARDY BOYS, AN ARCHWAY PAPERBACK
and colophon are registered trademarks of Simon & Schuster Inc.

THE HARDY BOYS CASEFILES is a trademark
of Simon & Schuster Inc.

Cover art by Brian Kotzky

Printed in the U.S.A.

FINAL GAMBIT

Chapter

1

"YOU KNOW, I could get used to this," Joe Hardy declared to his older brother Frank, who was sitting next to him on the plane. "It's Friday afternoon, and instead of being in school, we're flying to Las Vegas so you can compete in the National Teen Computer Chess Championship. If our friends could see us now!"

"Mmm," Frank mumbled. He had his nose buried in a book on advanced chess moves and was playing out some of the moves on a notebook computer set up on his tray.

"It's too bad the chess competition's on the weekend," Joe added. "We only get to miss today and Monday. Of course, the officials could decide to extend the competition. Then we'd be forced to stay all next week!"

Joe waited for a reaction, but Frank only reached out with his hand and made a move on his computer. Joe watched a castle move several squares straight up the board on the computer screen. Then he grabbed a plastic cup of soda from his tray, flipped the tray into its upright position, and half turned in his seat to try to distract his brother.

"Earth to Frank Hardy," Joe said, flipping his blond hair off his forehead. At seventeen, Joe was only a year younger than Frank, but at times he felt Frank acted like a boring old man. "I would think that if you don't know the moves by now, it's too late to learn them."

"That's ridiculous," Frank said, raising his eyes from the screen for the first time. Joe could see now that his brother's face looked drawn and tired from concentrating so hard. His brown hair was mussed up from absentmindedly taking swipes at it while working. "It's never too late to add programming, Joe," Frank said seriously. "Think about it. The computer I'm going to play chess against knows nothing but an enormous number of possible moves—whatever's been programmed into its software, right? Well, if I put more information into my own computer," he added, tapping his forehead, "I might save a game or two at the last minute. Besides, this book I'm practicing from is designed to help players think creatively—something the computer can't do."

"Whatever you say." Joe glanced down at Frank's chess book. The heading at the top of the page Frank was studying read, "Going for the Gambit." "Football's more my style. What does that mean—'going for the gambit'? Is it like making a first down?"

Frank was obviously surprised. "You don't know what a gambit is?"

Joe flushed. "If I knew, I'd have won the district chess championship instead of you, right? So just tell me."

Frank closed the book, but held his place with a finger. "A gambit's when one side, usually the white, starts the game by sacrificing one piece to lure the competition into a trap." He pressed a button on his computer keyboard, and the chess game on the screen was replaced with a newly set-up board. "For example, I might sacrifice a pawn or even two in the first moves to free my bishop," Frank said, expertly demonstrating on the computer. "My move would force you to move your knight out of my way so I could go after your queen. I might not win immediately, but I could confuse the computer and buy time for a later victory."

Frank started to continue, but Joe interrupted him with an enormous yawn. "Sounds great," Joe said, stretching. "I guess if anyone can beat that computer in Las Vegas, you can. Listen, I'm going for a walk. These long flights can really take it out of us more active types."

As Frank returned to his book, Joe unbuckled his seat belt and wandered down the aisle of the DC-10. It was weird, traveling as Frank's sidekick instead of being a major player, and Joe felt oddly restless. Sons of the famous detective, Fenton Hardy, and experienced detectives themselves, Frank and Joe had traveled all over the world on cases, but this trip was just for Frank. He had entered the nationwide computer chess competition on his own and had asked Joe to keep him company. Joe wasn't sure what he'd do once they arrived in Las Vegas and Frank became involved in his competition.

As though in answer to his question, his eyes rested on a beautiful woman with long dark hair, staring out the window with a bored expression. Her full mouth, dark brown eyes, and athletic build convinced Joe that she was a show girl on her way back to her job in Las Vegas. He walked faster down the aisle toward her row, sank into the empty seat beside her, and turned to start a friendly conversation.

His speech froze in his throat when he saw an infant sleeping in the woman's lap. Joe next saw the enormous diamond on the ring finger of her left hand. Joe realized now that she was in her late twenties, not eighteen or nineteen as he had thought.

"Oops," Joe muttered as the woman turned to him. "Uh, wrong seat."

Better luck next time, Joe told himself nervously as he vaulted out of the seat and started back through the plane. *Next time I'll check the ring finger first.*

Moving on, Joe caught the eye of a blond girl sitting at the back of the plane. She was alone, and it looked to Joe as if she was smiling at him! He caught his breath. The girl was incredibly beautiful. As she looked back down at a book or magazine in her lap, he noted how her long golden hair cascaded over her shoulders and framed a face so smooth that Joe knew she was not much older than he was.

Maybe this time I'm in luck, he told himself as he wandered down the aisle and came to a stop beside the girl.

Joe cleared his throat to get her attention.

To his surprise, the girl jumped in fright, slamming her book shut.

"Oh!" she said, her face blanching almost to white. "Sorry. I thought you were—"

"Thought I was who?" Joe pointed at the seat beside her. "Do you mind if I sit down?"

"Of course not," she replied, embarrassed. "It would be great to have someone to talk to. I'm feeling kind of—well, edgy, I guess."

"I'm Joe Hardy." He sat down and extended his hand. She shook it gratefully. "What's so scary?" Joe asked. "Does flying make you nervous?"

"Beth Cornelius. No, I like flying, actually. I just—well, I was afraid I was being followed."

At these words, Joe's ears pricked up. This sounded like a puzzle waiting to be solved, and nothing got Joe's attention like a mystery. He chuckled to show Beth she had nothing to fear from him. "Who'd follow you on a plane?" he asked. "Did you steal soap from the washroom or something?"

Beth frowned, offended. "This is serious," she said. "I'm talking about my father. He's a very powerful man and has connections everywhere. If he knew I was on this plane he'd send one of his men to take me back to New York."

"Why? You're old enough to fly alone, aren't you?"

"Eighteen," Beth stated. "But the problem is, I'm going to Las Vegas to meet my fiancé. We're getting married next week, and my dad hates him."

Joe's smile faded. "Oh," he mumbled. Then he added silently to himself, Oops.

"He'd do anything to stop us from getting married," Beth continued, not noticing Joe's reaction. "When you showed up, I thought you were working for him at first. But now I know I was wrong," she assured him. "Daddy would never hire someone so young."

Joe felt his face redden again. "I'm probably older than you think," he said. "Anyway, I don't even know who your father is. My brother's playing in a chess competition in Las Vegas, and I'm tagging along. It's sponsored by an electronic games outfit, and the object is to beat the company's computer at chess. Frank's already won the Northeastern District competitions, and I think he's going to win the nationals."

Beth nodded. "Right. The computer chess finals. My fiancé works in a hotel in Las Vegas, and he wasn't sure he could get me a room because so many people would be in town to see the playoffs."

"They will?" Joe said incredulously. "To watch *chess?* Unbelievable!"

Beth laughed. "I guess people will watch practically anything."

Just then the pilot announced that the plane was getting ready to land and asked all passengers to return to their seats.

Just my luck, she's getting married, Joe thought gloomily. I hope this isn't an omen for the weekend.

"It was great meeting you, Joe," Beth said, giving him a little kiss on the cheek.

"Y-yeah," he stammered. "Good luck with your, uh, wedding."

Joe returned quickly to his seat, smiling about that kiss. Maybe Beth was a little bit attracted to him after all. He sank down next to his brother and buckled his seat belt.

Frank put away his book and computer and turned to Joe. "Where have you been?" he asked.

"Making friends," Joe answered cheerfully. "With one gorgeous girl."

"That's nice," Frank said, preoccupied.

Poor Frank, Joe thought as the plane went into its final descent. He was so nervous about the contest he wasn't even interested in a girl. But then, he had his girlfriend, Callie Shaw, back home to keep him company.

As the plane landed at McCarran International Airport, Joe and Frank sat silently thinking their own thoughts.

Joe was soon distracted, though, as the Hardys entered Las Vegas's unusual airport. He stared at the rows of slot machines and the crowds of flashily dressed gamblers rushing for the exits. "Wow," he said as a six-foot-tall woman in sequins, feathers, and a four-foot headdress tottered by on spike-heeled shoes carrying a sign for a local hotel. "This may be my kind of town after all."

"Huh?" Frank said, blinking as he searched for the baggage area.

"Frank, wake up!" Joe said, losing patience at last. "You're in Fun Town, U.S.A. Loosen up a little! Anyway, who cares if you win a stupid chess competition if you're not going to have a good time?"

"I have to focus," Frank insisted as they waited for their luggage to appear on the airport carousel. Another show girl strutted past him, but again Frank failed to notice her. "I plan to be the best, Joe,'' he said. "I don't even care about the ten thousand dollars in prize money. I just want to be the best.''

"Ten thousand dollars?" Joe asked. "You never mentioned that before.''

"Didn't I?" Frank replied. "Anyway, I really want to win this. Every computer company in the world will want to hire me after I graduate from college if I do.''

Joe couldn't take it anymore. "But, Frank, you won't be out of college for years, and we're in Las Vegas right now!"

Frank smiled. "I know. That's why I wanted you to come along. I knew you'd have a great time here. Why don't you go find that girl you met? You did say something about a girl, didn't you?''

"She's engaged," Joe said gloomily. "She's here to meet her fiancé.''

As he spoke, a fall of blond hair flashed by in the crowd, and Joe caught a glimpse of Beth. She was hurrying toward the exit with her luggage as fast as she could, nervously glancing over her shoulder every few seconds.

Joe watched the sliding glass doors close behind her after she stepped outside. Beth was checking first one way, then the other. Finally she gripped her bags, turned left, and vanished into the crowd.

"She really is in trouble," Joe said to himself.

Frank groaned. "Don't say that, Joe. I don't have time for trouble this trip."

"Okay, fine," Joe said. "If you don't have the time to help some poor helpless girl, that's okay—"

"Joe!" Frank snapped, reaching for one of their suitcases. "Enough!"

That would have been the end of the discussion—except for the scream from outside that cut through the noise of the airport. Joe's eyes widened, and Frank froze for an instant.

"What was that?" Joe asked as the scream came again. It was a woman's scream—shrill and piercing, even though it was muffled by a wall of glass windows. "It's Beth!"

"Oh, no," Frank started to say as Joe ran for the sliding glass doors. He pushed past other passengers, positive that Frank would be right behind him.

"I knew it!" Joe yelled as he burst through the doorway. "Frank, look!"

Frank pulled up at his brother's side just as the scream sounded a third time. Joe pointed to the far end of the line of cars in the pickup area. A young blond woman was being shoved into a dusty old yellow sedan. The man pushing her into the car was turned halfway around, but Joe could see that he had a burly build and a mustache, and he wore black gloves.

"It *is* Beth!" Joe shouted. "Come on, Frank! We've got to save her!"

Chapter

2

"WATCH OUT!" Frank yelled as his brother sprinted out into traffic to stop the yellow car so it couldn't pull out. Tires squealed and horns honked as cars swerved to avoid hitting Joe. Frank raced along the sidewalk, keeping pace with his brother. They were approaching the car from two sides now.

"Joe! They're getting away!" The driver of the yellow car gunned the engine, pulled out in front of a bus, and swerved into the far left lane. Joe had figured out the driver's plan and leapt into the left lane in front of the sedan. Frank, on the sidewalk still, worked his way around a large family surrounded by luggage.

"No!" Frank yelled when he could see Joe again. While onlookers screamed, the sedan barreled toward Joe. Obviously the driver didn't care if he knocked Joe to the ground.

Frank raced out into the street, trying to reach Joe before the sedan did. Making a desperate leap, Frank managed to push his brother to the side of the road at the same instant the sedan whooshed by, emitting heat and fumes.

Frank and Joe fell to the pavement, ignoring the crowd of staring tourists as they watched the sedan dart down the road to the airport exit. "I got the license plate number," Frank announced to his brother, making a mental note of the numbers and letters. "It's a Nevada plate. The police can trace it easily, so there's no need for you to kill yourself over this!"

"Oh, yeah?" panted Joe, standing up and brushing himself off. "So where's an officer?" Before Frank could answer, Joe had run off again, obviously hoping to catch up with the sedan at the exit.

Frank looked back toward the airport, but despite all the honking horns there wasn't a police officer in sight. He did spot a man in a chauffeur's uniform, though, leaning back with his elbows on the hood of a shiny black limo. He was holding a printed sign that bore one word: Hardy.

Great, Frank said to himself. The competition people must have sent a car to take me to the hotel.

He ran over to the car and announced to the driver, "I'm Hardy. Let's go."

The chauffeur, who was only a few years older than Frank, checked a small notebook. "Frank Hardy?"

"For the chess match, right," Frank said breathlessly. The chauffeur finally opened the rear door for him, but Frank yanked open the driver's door and slid in behind the wheel.

"Hey, you can't do that!" the chauffeur protested as Frank turned the key and gunned the engine.

"Emergency!" Frank yelled. "I'll be back as soon as I can." He shoved the transmission into Drive. The limo roared away, leaving the chauffeur on the curb.

"Oh, great!" Frank muttered as he neared the airport exit and saw that the traffic was hopelessly snarled. "What a time for a traffic jam."

As other drivers honked their horns impatiently, Frank craned his neck out the window and saw the yellow car near the front of the line preparing to enter a major highway. Someone leapt a fence beside the road near the yellow sedan and raced toward the car.

"Joe!" Frank yelled, leaning out the window to see better. It was obvious to Frank that Joe didn't have a chance. Joe was fast, but even the best runner couldn't keep up with a car going at full speed.

"I guess it's up to me, then," Frank muttered

as he spun the steering wheel hard to the left and stepped on the gas. Horns honked as the limo bolted over a concrete barricade that separated the access road from the parking lot and zipped toward the exit.

He saw it too late—the thick wooden bar that separated the parking lot from the access road was down. The limo was headed straight for it.

"No way to stop in time!" Frank shouted as he aimed the limo straight for the bar. The black car sheared through it, then shot onto the highway.

"This car isn't bad," Frank admitted to himself as he stepped on the accelerator again, pursuing the sedan down the highway. He could see Joe running along the shoulder up ahead, slowing from a sprint to a hard jog. As the limo approached Joe, Frank punched a switch to open the rear passenger door. He hit the horn.

"Hey, Joe!" he shouted through the open passenger window. Without taking his eyes off the yellow sedan, Joe nodded and moved closer to the lane of traffic. As Frank caught up with Joe, he slowed the limo to keep pace with him. Joe reached for the open rear door.

"All right!" Frank shouted as Joe gripped the top of the inside of the door. Grunting, Joe lifted his feet off the ground. The door started to swing closed under his weight, sending him back toward the car. Joe braced his feet against the door, then let go with his hands and kicked. He fell onto the backseat. The door whipped open once more, bounced back, and slammed shut.

"I was beginning to think you wouldn't make it," Frank said, relieved.

Joe scrambled into the front seat and slipped on his seat belt. "Yeah, but I haven't caught them yet. Nice car. Where'd you get it?"

"Oh, it was just sitting there waiting for me." Frank cocked an eyebrow, glancing at the two-way radio under the dashboard. "Try to get us some backup while I see if I can catch that sedan."

Joe took the microphone from the radio and hit a button on it twice with his thumb. "Ten-four. Is anybody out there?"

A voice crackled from the speaker. "Car twelve, what's going on? Andy, didn't your charter show up?"

"This isn't Andy," Joe said. "This is Joe Hardy. My brother and I borrowed this car to chase down a kidnapper in a canary yellow sedan. Think we could get some local help on this?"

"You guys cops?" the voice asked.

"Um, sort of. We're heading— Well, I'm not sure which direction. What road are you on when you pull left out of the airport?"

The voice hardened. "You're on Las Vegas Boulevard. The Strip, man. Did you say your name was Hardy? Frank Hardy?"

"That's my brother. I'm Joe."

"I don't care who you are. If you're not a cop, get that car back here right now or we report it stolen! You got me?"

"Sorry," Joe said. "We can't do that. See what you can do about getting the local police out here, okay?" He hung up the microphone and switched off the radio.

"Think we made him angry?" Joe asked, grinning.

"I think that's the car up there," Frank said, pointing to a yellow dot far ahead. The dot made a sharp left, and Frank took the same turn, concentrating on catching the sedan.

"Wow," he heard Joe comment as they moved along the two-lane road that cut across flat brown desert. "This car can really cook! We're bound to catch up with them in the long run."

"Yeah." Frank kept his eyes locked on the yellow sedan as the distance between the two cars narrowed. "We don't know how good the driver is, though. And if we do catch them, we don't know how violent they're willing to get. We could be driving into a shooting gallery."

"Thanks for reminding me," Joe said as the limo closed in on the sedan. Then Joe's voice turned grimmer. "Something's up."

Joe was right, Frank realized. The sedan was purposely slowing down, allowing them to get close enough for Frank to make out three, not two, figures in the car.

"The blond girl in the back is Beth," Joe said.

16

"The guy in the front passenger seat is the kidnapper. I didn't get a good look at the driver. All I can make out now is his silhouette. But I bet those guys were hired by Beth's father. She told me she was scared he'd try to stop her from seeing her fiancé."

Frank nodded. The glare of the afternoon sun against the sedan's windows made it hard to see inside. "They seem to be looking for something," Frank said, catching the odd motions of the heads in the other car. "This seems too violent and public to have been ordered by that girl's own father. They could just be kidnappers," Frank suggested. "If Beth's father is rich, they might have grabbed her for ransom."

"I don't know—" Joe didn't have time to continue. Frank had steered the limo onto another, even narrower side road in pursuit of the yellow car.

"What on earth is that?" said Joe, sounding startled. Frank, too, was staring at what appeared to be a miniature Las Vegas—a lot filled with billboards and marquees, neon signs and stacked automobiles, like a bizarre shrine right in the middle of the Nevada desert. A chainlink fence surrounded the area, but the gate was open.

"I've seen junkyards before, but never like this," Frank said with a whistle. "Wait—I've read about these. Neon graveyards, they're called.

17

When casinos close or redecorate, the old signs and stuff have to go. Most of the stuff gets taken out here to the desert. I've heard of guys who hook up all the old neon signs so they can light them up at night.''

"Looks like that's where the kidnappers are going," Joe said as the yellow car turned into the neon graveyard. "Think we can take them?"

"I guess we'll find out," answered Frank. In a little while he, too, turned into the graveyard through the gate.

"Wow. Now I know why they call it a graveyard," Joe remarked.

Frank nodded grimly. As they moved along the narrow drive, the lot was as silent as a tomb. Frank strained his ears to pick up any sound as he steered past huge stacks of molded glass tubing. The only sound besides the soft rumble of the luxury car's engine was the whistle of the desert wind. The kidnappers had vanished.

"Spooky, isn't—" Joe said. He was interrupted by a sudden loud hum. All the neon signs in the lot had been switched on, and the space was lit by an eerie red and gold glow. Before the brothers could react to the sight, a blast split the air.

"The tire's blown!" Frank cried, as the limo's rear tire exploded. The steering wheel wobbled, and Frank slammed his foot down on the brake. But the loose desert sand shifted under the three good tires, and the car skidded and spun.

"The brakes have locked up!" Frank shouted. "Brace yourself, Joe. We're going to crash!"

Ahead of them loomed a huge neon hand holding four giant playing cards that blinked on and off. Frank and Joe cried out as the limo smashed into the ace of spades and came to a halt halfway through the sign.

"You okay?" Frank asked Joe in the silence that followed. Around them the other three cards continued to blink on and off, humming softly.

"Yeah," Joe said. "Good thing I was wearing my seat belt. Think we can get out of here?"

"Let's try," Frank said.

He reached for the door handle, his fingers almost squeezing it when Joe yelled, "Frank, wait!"

At the same instant Joe yelled, Frank realized what the trouble was. Electricity was making the sign hum and the neon cards flash. The car was sitting in the middle of the sign, which meant they were in an electrical current. . . .

All these thoughts went through Frank's mind in the split second it took for his fingers to brush against the metal door handle. By then, it was too late to pull back, and the electric shock jolted Frank sideways and into Joe.

"No!" Frank heard his brother cry as darkness fell over his eyes.

Chapter

3

"HOLD ON, FRANK." Joe gingerly pushed his unconscious brother away until his head rested against the back of the seat. In falling against him like that, Frank had nearly knocked Joe against the passenger door and shocked him as well.

Joe held the back of his hand under Frank's nose. Frank was breathing, strong and steady. The jolt had knocked him out, but he'd be all right. Frank must have only grazed the metal door handle. Joe knew full contact would have fried him.

"Well, now we know what kind of people we're dealing with," Joe muttered when no one came to turn off the signs. Joe wondered how he and Frank would ever get out of the electrified limo. It was only a matter of time before one of them accidentally touched metal, and Joe didn't like the idea of dying in the middle of the desert. There was no hope of rescue. Only Beth and the kidnappers knew they were there. It could be days before anyone came to the neon graveyard.

"Frank," Joe said. His brother didn't move. "Frank!" he said again, louder. Still nothing.

He pinched Frank's nose closed. For a moment, Frank still didn't move. Then he coughed and sputtered, and Joe let go of his nose and held him close to keep him from flailing.

Frank blinked, bringing his gasping under control. He was extremely pale. "Joe? What happened?" he asked.

"You caught a few volts. I had to choke you to wake you up."

"Thanks a lot," said Frank, still extremely dazed. "Well, that's that, I guess. Time to get out of here and go get our luggage."

"Good idea," Joe said, humoring him. Any suggestions?"

"As long as we're insulated, we're okay. We can break windows, but we still have to get past the metal to get out. If only we could take insulation with us—" Frank snapped his fingers, fully alert now. "Move the front seat all the way up and climb into the backseat. Now."

Joe did what Frank said. Frank followed him to the back. The boys sat side by side and grabbed hold of the back of the front seat and began to rock it back and forth.

Joe's palms tingled from the electric current as he pushed and pulled on the back of the seat to work it free of its moorings. Beside him, Frank chanted, "One, two, three, now!"

Grunting with effort, both boys yanked back at the same time. The seat back came loose and fell into their laps.

"Whew!" Joe held on to the slab of wood and padding. "And to think some people complain about bad workmanship in cars these days."

"Save the jokes until we're safe," said Frank.

"Okay," Joe replied. He and Frank turned the seat back sideways and aimed it at the rear windshield like a battering ram.

"Ready?" Frank said.

"You bet." Joe lifted his side of the seat back and helped Frank ram it through the rear window.

The glass shattered into a single crumpled sheet, and the seat back fell onto the trunk of the limo. Carefully Joe slid the seat back so it straddled the whole length of the trunk.

"Age before beauty," Joe told Frank.

Frank climbed through the broken window and somersaulted down the seat back while Joe held it firmly in place. Frank landed in a heap in the dirt, inches beyond the electrified car.

"I just thought of something, Joe," Frank said. "How are you going to get out? You balanced the seat for me, but I can't get back to balance it for you."

"A fine time to think of that," Joe said. "But never fear. Here goes!"

"Joe! No!" Frank yelled, but there was no way to stop him now. Crouching for maximum leverage, Joe pushed off through the rear windshield and belly flopped onto the seat back. The impact sent the seat back sliding right off the trunk. Riding the seat back like a surfboard, Joe landed with a laugh at Frank's feet.

Frank stared at Joe as if he were out of his mind, which only made Joe laugh harder. Gradually, Frank began to chuckle, too.

They were still laughing when Joe heard clicks erupting all around them. Joe's grin froze. He knew the sounds of gun hammers clicking into place.

With a feeling of dread, Joe looked up to see a tall middle-aged man in a gray suit step warily forward from a ring of police officers with drawn revolvers. The cop trained his .38 on the Hardys. At first Joe thought the policeman was bald, but as he approached, Joe could make out blond hair cut close to his head. Joe shuddered. The officer's grim scowl didn't foretell a bright future for the boys.

"Hands up," the man said in a southwestern drawl. "Sergeant Hirsch, Las Vegas Police. You boys are under arrest."

*   *   *

"Honest, sir, we were just trying to save the girl," Joe insisted a couple of hours later when Sergeant Hirsch reentered the interrogation room riffling a small stack of papers in his hand. "We didn't fly all the way down here to smash up somebody's junkyard."

"It doesn't matter anymore, anyway," the tall, wiry sergeant said unhappily. "You boys are off the hook. The junkyard owners don't want to pursue trespassing or vandalism charges, and the car company says their insurance will cover damages. No one's charging you with anything. Your chauffeur is checking with a lawyer, though," he added, glaring at Frank, "to see if there's anything he can sue you for."

"We had a driver?" Joe said to Frank.

Hirsch cut him off. "I also checked with the police in Bayport, of course. They give you a clean bill of health. And the chess people verify that Frank is enrolled in their tournament."

"Does that mean we can go?" asked Frank.

"Not so fast," Hirsch said. "I still have a lot of unanswered questions. At the top of the list is this one: how come you just happened to get into a conversation with a young lady on your plane minutes before she was kidnapped?"

"What's that supposed to mean?" Joe was getting tired of Hirsch and his accusations. "I already told you, I thought she was cute and sat down to talk to her. That's all. It was just a coincidence!"

"That's what you claim, bright boy," Hirsch said. "But Bayport sent your records, and I know you two have been up to your necks in other people's business before. If I were a gambling man I'd bet there's lots you've been involved with that didn't even make it onto your record. You aren't going to convince me your connection to a kidnapping victim is a coincidence."

"You don't gamble?" Frank said, trying to distract him.

Hirsch scowled. "Gambling's for suckers." He slammed the stack of paper down on the table and glared at the Hardys. "I want you to know I've notified the girl's father that she was taken. He's on his way here now in his private plane."

Hirsch added gravely, "Mr. Cornelius is a powerful man, not only in New York but in Las Vegas and several other cities, too. He's been known to get nasty, especially when his daughter's safety is threatened. That means that if you two are involved in this kidnapping in *any* way, Cornelius will get wind of it sooner or later. And then you'll be hoping for me to come to your rescue. Understand?"

The Hardys stared at him without answering.

"Okay, you can go," Hirsch grumbled, motioning them toward the door.

"Thanks," Frank said shortly. Joe didn't feel like saying even that much.

"A couple of other things," Hirsch added just before the Hardys reached the door. "That license number you read off the sedan? It doesn't exist."

"I know I read it right," Frank said. "How's that possible?"

Hirsch shrugged. "Car thieves take two different plates, cut them in half, and weld the pieces together to get new license numbers."

"So you think car thieves are involved?" Joe asked.

Hirsch shrugged. "Who knows? Your kidnapper friends might have bought the plates from someone. You're staying at the Camelot, right?"

"The kidnappers aren't our friends," Frank replied curtly. "And, yes, we are."

Hirsch nodded. "Stay at the Camelot, boys. And I mean *stay* there. Don't leave the building. If you should get bored hanging around your hotel, just remember that you're too young to gamble legally. I have officers everywhere."

"We don't gamble," Joe said.

"You amateur detectives are the worst kind of gamblers," Hirsch replied. "Other people gamble with money. You gamble with lives."

The police car dropped Frank and Joe off at the front entrance of the Camelot. Joe had never seen anything like the gigantic hotel built to look like a castle from the days of King Arthur. And when they stepped inside, Joe noticed that the employees were dressed as knights or ladies-in-waiting. The men wore lightweight suits of armor and the women wore long, flowing gowns.

"Wow. I feel as if we just stepped onto a movie set," Joe said, staring at the bustling crowds in the enormous lobby as Frank checked them in. Nearby, a sunken room, larger than a football field, held dozens of rows of slot machines. The pitlike area was filled with guests madly feeding coins into the machines.

Joe turned away from the sight to accept the room key Frank tossed to him. "You go up and wait for the luggage," Frank said. "The desk clerk said she'd send someone to the airport to get it for us."

"Where will you be?" Joe asked.

"I'm going to get some money. The desk clerk says there's a bank with a money machine at the far end of the lobby. I might take a quick look around the place, too."

Joe nodded. "Maybe you should get a little extra cash." He pointed to the slot machines and to the banner that hung over the room.

" 'Slots Competition—One Million Dollar Grand Prize,' " Joe read out loud. "Sounds interesting!"

"You told Hirsch we didn't gamble," Frank reminded him.

Joe winced. "We don't, but, Frank, a million dollars! Why should only one of us be in a tournament here, right?"

Frank laughed and began to walk away.

Joe took one last longing look at the banners before crossing the lobby to the bank of elevators. He rode up to the twenty-second floor.

"This is it?" Joe muttered as he entered their room. From the way the lobby was decorated, Joe realized, he'd been expecting more. The room was nice enough, with two beds, a television, and a small balcony. But while the rest of the hotel was done up as a medieval castle, their room had only plain bedspreads and paintings of flowers and ducks that wouldn't have looked out of place in the Hardys' house.

"Oh, well," he said, and sprawled out on one of the beds. It was only early evening, but he was tired after the long flight and the excitement at the airport. How can I complain when it's free—and I'm in Fun City, U.S.A.? he thought as he drifted off.

It seemed only an instant later when Joe awoke to the sound of someone rapping on the door. "Frank?" he called sleepily, sitting up. He glanced out the window. It was nearly dark outside. Joe realized he must have slept for over an hour.

The rapping sounded again. "Okay, Frank, hold your horses," Joe grumbled, getting up to open the door. Just as he unlatched it and gave it a pull, the door slammed open, knocking Joe back against the wall.

"Hey!" Joe sputtered as a pair of rough hands

grabbed him by the collar. Instinctively, Joe punched at the face in front of him, but the blow bounced off the man's jaw, and Joe found himself staring into dark, blank eyes.

"Shut up!" The man's hand moved like lightning and cracked against the side of Joe's head. Dazed, Joe felt himself being dragged across the floor. A door was slid open. Then the heat of the outdoors was on his face, and his feet were dangling into empty space.

Joe opened his eyes and gasped. His attacker was dangling him at arm's length off the balcony, holding on to nothing but the front of Joe's shirt. This guy was practically a giant, Joe realized.

"Hello there, Joe!" Another man appeared behind the attacker. The short, middle-aged newcomer was suavely dressed in an expensive-looking sports jacket. Joe squinted and took in his receding blond hairline and thin, fine-boned face with glasses perched on his nose. Joe tried to figure out why the man seemed so familiar.

"This is Elroy," the newcomer said, waving a thumb at the giant dangling Joe over the balcony. "You can call me Mr. Cornelius. My friends in the Vegas police department tell me you know my daughter."

Joe said nothing. So this was Beth's father. Joe felt his stomach do a somersault as he continued to dangle out over the railing.

As though he knew what Joe was thinking,

29

Cornelius said, "The way I see it, Joe—may I call you Joe?—you have two choices. You can talk to me and take me to my daughter, or Elroy here can drop you twenty-two stories to that concrete drive below."

The man moved closer to the railing, watching Joe with a chilling smile. "Which will it be, kid?" he demanded casually. "A little chat with me, or certain death?"

Chapter

4

FRANK HARDY walked into the hotel room and stopped. It wasn't the first time he had found his brother's life hanging by a thread, but it sure wasn't what he'd expected right then.

"What's going on?" he asked, careful to give no sign of how scared he was.

The thug holding Joe cocked his head to see where the voice was coming from, and Mr. Cornelius turned slowly to reveal a sharklike smile stretched across his lips.

"This is Mr. Cornelius, Frank," Joe called from the balcony, covering up his fear with mock politeness. "You remember—Beth's father?"

Frank gave the well-dressed man another glance. Something about the name and face struck a familiar note, but Frank couldn't understand why. He was too worried about Joe to concentrate hard.

"You must be Joe's brother," Cornelius said, eyeing Frank. "The other kidnapper!"

"Hmmm?" Frank said, forcing himself to pay attention. "You'll have to explain that one. Maybe you could bring him back inside while you do." Frank nodded in Joe's direction. "Then we could talk about this in private. Otherwise, there could be a dozen witnesses downstairs who'll feel they have to interfere."

Cornelius smiled. "I like you, kid. You've got nerve." He snapped his fingers. "Okay, Elroy, reel the fish in."

Without a word, the muscleman dumped Joe on the balcony. Joe scrambled to his feet, and Elroy shoved him into the room behind Cornelius.

"Sit down," Cornelius ordered, pointing to two thickly padded chairs along a wall. When neither Frank nor Joe moved, he shouted, "Sit down!" leaving no doubt that they didn't have a choice.

"Now," he continued after the Hardys had taken their seats, "how about telling me what you did with my little girl?"

"We tried to get her back," Frank snapped. "Two men in a yellow sedan grabbed her. We chased them out into the desert."

Cornelius waved a hand in the air, dismissing Frank's statement. "What do you think I am, a moron? You're two total strangers who never met my daughter before today, and you risked your lives to save her from unknown kidnappers? Nobody, but nobody, would believe that one."

Frank checked out Joe, but neither of them said a word.

"Tell me the truth!" Cornelius shouted. Elroy took a menacing step toward the Hardys. "You're out of your league here, boys," Cornelius snarled. "I want answers, and they'd better be good. What is it? You don't think I'm smart enough for you—just because you're detectives?"

Frank flinched at the word, and Cornelius smiled. "Yeah, I had you checked out," he said. "Perfect front guys for a kidnapping—no cop in the country would arrest the sons of Fenton Hardy. How long have you low-rent creeps been working on this? Since New York? How'd you get my Beth on the plane, huh?"

"What's he talking about?" Joe asked Frank.

Frank shrugged. "I guess we'll find out."

"Oh, yeah." The smile slid from Cornelius's lips. "You'll find out. We'll all find out! Won't we, Elroy?"

"How?" Joe said. "You're going to torture us?"

The smile came back, slicker than before. "I don't think it's something we can pursue here, anyway. Escort them, Elroy."

Elroy grabbed Frank and Joe by the shoulders

33

and hauled them to their feet. "Let's go," he mumbled.

"Yes, sir!" Joe muttered as Elroy shoved them to the door.

"You'll never get us out of the building," Frank pointed out as the four of them moved down the deserted hallway to wait for the elevator. "We'd have to go past too many people to get to the door."

"Smart kid," Cornelius sneered. "That's the sort of thinking I'd expect from a big detective like you. I guess it's a good thing we're not leaving the Camelot, then."

The elevator arrived, and Elroy pushed the Hardys inside. Cornelius stepped in after them, took a key from his pocket, and stuck it into the control panel. Frank felt his stomach sink when he saw the key.

"What's the key for?" Joe demanded.

"You want to tell him or should I?" Cornelius said to Frank. When Frank didn't answer, Cornelius continued. "See, kid, this hotel has all kinds of luxury features. Rock stars, politicians—anyone who needs quiet and security and can afford to rent it—can get the whole top floor all to themselves. You can't get up there without a key, though. And once the hotel rents you the floor, even their own security people don't get a copy of the key. Perfect privacy, you might say."

Frank couldn't miss the implied threat. Once he and Joe walked onto that top floor, they would simply vanish, unless they told Cornelius what he wanted to know.

Cornelius turned the key, and the elevator began rising slowly. Just then Frank remembered where he'd seen the man before. "Wait a minute!" he said. "You're *Jerome* Cornelius, aren't you! I saw a report on you once." Frank strained to recall what he had read. "You're some kind of cutthroat businessman. You specialize in pressuring up-and-coming businesses into selling out to you, and then you sell off all their assets for a quick buck."

"I've never been convicted of anything illegal," Cornelius said sharply.

"No, but you've been indicted a dozen times for strong-arming people into doing business with you. Funny how witnesses change their stories after a hospital stay," Frank said while Joe eyed the slowly changing floor indicator above the door.

"Keep it up, pal," Cornelius snapped. "You'll find out all about strong-arming."

"Let me ask you something," Frank said. "What makes you so sure we kidnapped Beth?"

Cornelius spun around and raised a fist to Frank. "I know you're involved in this caper because no one could stumble into it by accident, see?"

He pulled back his arm and lowered it, still glaring at Frank. "How much did you figure on hitting me up for?" Cornelius demanded. "What was the ransom going to be?"

"How much have you got?" Joe said. His eyes, and Frank's, were on the lights above the door that indicated they had reached the top floor. Frank's gaze dropped to meet Joe's. Joe gave a tiny nod, indicating that he had a plan.

As the elevator stopped and the doors slid open, Joe yelled, "Now!"

He spun, driving his fist as hard as he could into Elroy's ear. Frank picked up his cue and swiftly swept his arm around, driving his palm flat against Elroy's other ear. The big man's eyes snapped wide open and then went blank. As the shock to his eardrums settled in, Elroy dropped to his knees, his hands over his ears.

Cornelius plunged one hand inside his suitcoat and drew out a small pistol.

"Joe!" Frank said, punching the Open Door button on the control panel.

Joe drove his shoulder into Cornelius as if he were plowing through a running back on a football field and knocked the older man out the door. Frank grabbed Joe and yanked him back in, then hit the Close Door button.

As Cornelius got to one knee and started to take aim, the doors slid closed.

"What do we do about Godzilla?" Joe yelled. Behind them, Elroy had staggered to his feet, hands still cupping his ears.

Frank punched the Express button. The elevator dropped like a stone, bypassing all the floors to the lobby.

"Keep him down," Frank ordered. All they needed was a minute, until the doors opened and they could escape into the immense hotel lobby.

That was too long, though. Elroy jumped up and lunged at Joe, clamping his huge hands around the boy's neck.

"Frank!" Joe's face reddened as Elroy's grip tightened.

Frank hurled himself against the big man's back, driving an elbow into Elroy's spine. Unfazed, Elroy lifted Joe up by the neck with one hand and turned to glare at Frank. A soft, guttural growl came from Elroy's throat. His free hand shot out and grabbed Frank by the neck as well.

Just as Elroy was lifting Frank up, too, the elevator doors opened.

Outside in the lobby, a crowd was waiting to enter. A woman in the crowd screamed.

For a moment Elroy hesitated. Frank felt the man's grip loosen around his neck.

"Kick!" Frank gurgled at Joe, not even certain the sound would come out. He brought his knees up and braced his feet against Elroy's chest. Joe did the same. Then they shoved out with their feet, straightening their legs until they were fully extended. Elroy slammed back against the elevator wall, and Frank and Joe sailed backward, going into twin flips as they hit the floor.

"Joe," Frank gasped, glancing over his shoulder. Elroy was after them already. "If we get into a fight here we'll have the hotel security staff down on us. I don't want to get bumped out of the competition."

"Gee, I'm glad you thought of that," Joe said sarcastically, ignoring the crowds staring at them as they took off running. Ahead of them a young man in a medieval squire's costume hurried through a door, letting it swing wide open. On the door was a sign: Employees Only.

"In here, Frank," Joe yelled. He grabbed the door and held it open. Frank followed Joe in, then slammed the door and bolted it behind him. It was a solid steel door, he noted, strong enough to keep even Elroy out.

Frank sank to one knee to catch his breath. He noticed he was kneeling in dirt instead of on tile or carpet. Then he became aware of a noise like thunder—a rolling, staccato sound that seemed to be growing louder.

Frank raised his head, alarmed.

A horse in medieval armor was bearing down on them. Astride the horse was a knight, also in full armor.

"W-wait a minute," Frank stammered, wondering if he'd been knocked unconscious and was dreaming. The knight's lance shone in the overhead light, and Frank could actually taste the dust kicked up by the horse's hooves.

"It's real!" Frank heard Joe shout as both boys whirled in the opposite direction to see another knight on horseback charging from the other side.

"You bet it's real!" Frank yelled. "And we're caught in the middle!"

Chapter

5

JOE SHOVED HIS BROTHER back against the wall out of the way of one rider. He stumbled when he started to run himself and fell to the dirt floor.

The first horse was safely past, but the second one was thundering toward him. Eight hundred pounds of beast, man, and metal were bearing down on him. The horse lengthened its pace just before it reached Joe's prone body.

This is it, Joe thought, closing his eyes. But, miraculously, the horse and rider sailed over him without touching him. Both riders stopped at the far end of the room and turned back to the Hardys, their horses stamping the ground impatiently.

Somewhere someone yelled, "Security!"

The space they were in was surrounded by high wooden walls. Beyond the walls, people sat at tables feasting on plates of meat, bread, and fruit. The people wore ordinary clothes and were staring at the Hardys in amazement.

It's a hotel restaurant, Joe realized. Customers were being entertained during their meal by knights jousting in a mock medieval tournament.

Frank and Joe had become unwelcome additions to the entertainment.

"Joe!" Frank whispered. "Let's get out of here!"

Joe hesitated. On the one hand, he knew that Elroy was probably just beyond that steel door. On the other hand, he thought, as he watched hotel security guards charge toward them, staying there could get them into more trouble. It might even cost Frank the chess championship. The electronic games company wasn't likely to want a juvenile delinquent as its award winner.

As Frank unbolted the door, Joe hoped Elroy had given up on them and gone back to Cornelius. His heart sank when a gruff voice greeted them as they reentered the hall.

"Hello, boys," said Elroy.

"Hi there, stranger," Joe quipped weakly. "Going up, I guess?"

"This is some place," Joe muttered to Frank as Elroy shoved the two of them into the penthouse from the elevator. He took in the floors and walls of polished marble. Electric lights designed like torches hung from the walls. The

41

suite seemed to wind on forever, a maze of rooms that finally led to a sunken living room framed with huge oak timbers.

"If the Camelot is a castle," Joe commented to his brother, "these are definitely the king's chambers."

Cornelius, relaxed and dressed now in a silk robe, sat watching the financial news on television. As Elroy nudged Frank and Joe into the room, Cornelius flashed them his toothy smile and patted a couch, signaling them to sit.

This time they sat right away.

"Don't look so glum, boys," Cornelius said cheerfully. "At least you get to see real luxury. Most people never get anywhere near a place like this."

He hit a button on the remote control, and the television clicked off. He pushed another button, and the television sank into the floor, instantly making the room appear even more elegant and spacious.

"You should take a look at my balcony," Cornelius continued. "You can see the whole city and the desert for miles around. The view is splendid at night."

"No, thanks," Joe said. "I've had enough of balconies for one day."

Cornelius laughed. "You never know, kid." Then his voice turned chilly. "Enough jokes. You two have thirty seconds to tell me where my little girl is, or you'll go air-surfing off my balcony. Elroy!''

Elroy stepped up behind Frank and Joe, not laying a hand on them but shoving them, couch and all, toward the balcony.

"Hey!" Joe yelled. "Watch it!"

"I can't hear you," Cornelius said. "Twenty seconds."

"You're wrong about all this," Frank said. "Just listen to me for a second!"

"Ten seconds," Cornelius said. Elroy shoved them again.

Just as Joe started to panic, a familiar voice floated in from the next room. "Anybody home?"

Cornelius and Elroy froze as Sergeant Hirsch stepped into the living room, holding his badge up for everyone to see. "Hirsch, LVPD. I hope I'm not interrupting anything."

"You're Hirsch, eh?" Cornelius growled. "I spoke with you on the phone. How did you get in here?"

Hirsch wiggled a key by its chain on his finger. It was obviously a duplicate of the key Cornelius had used in the elevator. Joe and Frank exchanged relieved glances as Cornelius's face grew red with anger.

"There's supposed to be only one key to this place," Cornelius protested.

"With all due respect, it's a bad idea to believe everything you read in brochures," Hirsch replied, nodding at the boys. "The hotels in this town prefer to cooperate with the police—especially when renting to a man of your reputation, Mr. Cornelius.''

Cornelius trembled with rage. In a low, barely controlled voice, he said, "Why are you here, Hirsch? Do you have news about my daughter?''

Hirsch pointed at Frank and Joe. "I'm here for them.''

"I don't think Mr. Cornelius will let us leave,'' Frank said. "He seems to think we kidnapped his daughter.''

Sergeant Hirsch looked surprised. "Why would he think that?''

Joe said pointedly, "Someone at the police station gave him that idea.''

Hirsch's eyes narrowed. "Mr. Cornelius, I can assure you that the Las Vegas Police do not suspect Frank or Joe Hardy of having taken part in the kidnapping. Our evidence only indicates that they made a mess of trying to prevent it, endangering the lives of others in the process.

"In fact,'' Hirsch continued, "the boys have agreed to use their detecting talents to help us in this investigation.''

Joe exchanged a surprised look with his brother. This was the first Joe had heard about the Las Vegas Police Department wanting help.

"I assure you, Mr. Cornelius, that the Hardys can help us find your daughter,'' the sergeant said. "Now, if you'll excuse us, we need some privacy to discuss the specifics of the case.''

"Are you keeping secrets from me?" Cornelius demanded.

"Of course not, sir," Hirsch said, herding the boys out of the room. "We'll be in touch as soon as we have news, sir. Meanwhile, I hope you enjoy your stay here—as always."

After they got into the elevator, Frank said, "Is this some good cop–bad cop routine you worked out with Cornelius? He threatens us if we don't talk. Then you show up to save us, and we go all soft for you and tell you what you want to know?"

"What do I want to know?" Hirsch said, inserting his key in the elevator control panel. "Do you have some information you haven't given me?"

"No," said Joe. "But no one believes us."

"I believe you," Hirsch said shortly. "Frankly, just about anyone who's an enemy of Jerome Cornelius is an ally of mine. And, no, I'm not working with the man. I'd need a very good reason to work with a gangster like that. But he is the girl's father, and he has a right to be involved in the case. Besides, you can see how concerned he is—he flew right here the instant I contacted him."

"By the way, how did you know where we were?" Frank asked.

"I was just going to get on an elevator in the lobby to go up to visit you when I saw that thug shove you into another elevator," Hirsch replied briskly. "When I saw it was going up, I watched to see where it stopped. It took me a few minutes to squeeze the extra key out of the desk clerk."

"Squeeze?" Joe said. "I thought you said the hotels cooperated with the police."

Hirsch chuckled. "In your dreams. Their customers come first. I understand that. But there's no reason Cornelius has to know."

"So, what was all that stuff about us working with you?"

"You are," Hirsch said. "On special assignment, if you're willing. Are you willing?"

Joe tried to read his brother's face. He couldn't. Frank was pursing his lips, thinking.

Finally Frank nodded.

"Okay," Joe said, too. "Frank's going to be busy with the chess competition, but I don't have much to do. I'll be glad to help. If you really need him, Frank will step in when he can."

"It's a deal," Hirsch said. "Be in my office at ten o'clock tomorrow morning. Meanwhile, I'll talk with Cornelius again to make sure he doesn't bother you. And thanks."

Thanks for what? Joe wondered. What did Hirsch want them to do?

Early the next morning Joe left Frank at the auditorium inside the Camelot where the contest

46

was to be held and hurried outside for his first walking tour of Las Vegas. It was a perfect day—warm, sunny, and dry. The bright green lawns around the hotels contrasted sharply with Joe's memory of his drive through the desert the day before.

He decided to walk all the way to the police station so he could see as much of Las Vegas as possible before Hirsch put him to work. Armed with a city map, he strode briskly along the wide sidewalk, amazed that no one else was out walking. Joe guessed they were all inside gambling already. Anyway, he thought, the hotels were so enormous that most tourists probably never went outside.

By the time Joe reached the police station, he was half blind from the glitz and glitter of fake volcanoes, centurion doormen, and the occasional couple in evening dress stumbling back in the morning light to their hotel. Feeling dazed, he approached the front desk and told the desk sergeant, "Joe Hardy to see Sergeant Hirsch, please."

The desk sergeant, a bulldog of a man, stared at Joe. "What was the name?"

"Joe Hardy," Joe repeated.

"Hardy," the desk sergeant said. He vanished down a hallway. A few seconds later he returned and pointed down the hall. "That way. You'll see him."

Joe walked down the hall. It was the cleanest

police station he had ever seen. Even the door-knobs were shined. It was, he thought, the least you'd expect from a city that depended completely on tourism for its income.

He came to a partly open door and saw Hirsch inside, leaning over a table speaking to someone Joe couldn't see. Joe pushed the door open.

He froze.

Sitting at the table in an elegant white suit was Jerome Cornelius, with Elroy hovering behind him like a monstrous shadow. On the table in front of Cornelius was a black leather briefcase.

"Hello, Joe," Hirsch said. "I trust we can all forget yesterday's unpleasantness. Please take a seat."

Joe sat down across from Cornelius. The older man glared at him, and Joe stared in return.

"Glad you could make it, Joe," Hirsch continued. "You're the cornerstone of our little plan."

"What plan?" Joe asked.

"Open the briefcase, Mr. Cornelius," Hirsch suggested.

Very reluctantly Cornelius opened it. All it contained was a single piece of paper.

Joe looked closer. The single piece of paper was a certified check—for one million dollars.

"You're the go-between, Joe," Hirsch said briskly, all business now. "You will deliver the ransom indirectly to the kidnappers. You and your brother are to open a joint savings account with this check, and then the kidnappers will withdraw the money later.''

"How can that work? No one can take money out of someone else's account," Joe said reasonably.

"I'm sure there'll be another set of instructions later. This is probably just a temporary plan to see if we follow directions and if the money is really deposited," Hirsch answered.

"Why me?" Joe could feel his pulse speed up at the thought of getting so deeply involved.

"You tell us, Hardy," Cornelius growled. "The police got a call from the kidnappers last night. They laid out the terms of the payoff—how, when, who."

"And they demanded that the ransom be delivered by you," Hirsch said softly.

Joe turned to the sergeant. "Please," he groaned, "tell me I'm dreaming!"

Chapter

6

"WELCOME, EVERYONE."

Frank shifted in his chair as an attractive young woman in a gray suit addressed the chess players in the auditorium of the Camelot Hotel. Both she and the players were on the stage. The young woman stood beside a minicomputer on an elaborate stand, and the seven young finalists sat at a crescent-shaped row of computer terminals, facing her. Behind them, rows of upholstered seats rose from the floor of the auditorium near the stage, almost to the ceiling in the rear.

To Frank's relief, the six other competitors, all winners from different districts around the country, looked as apprehensive as he felt as they settled into their places at the terminals. Above them hung giant video screens that would allow the audience to watch their chess games in progress. Frank was glad the young woman spoke with such assurance and in a gentle voice. Pretty, with short brown hair, she smiled at the teenage contestants, putting them a little more at ease.

"My name is Janet Lassen. The Rightway Electronics Corporation has asked me, as one of the Thinker's designers, to oversee this tournament," the woman continued. "Thank you for coming to this orientation session."

Frank nodded absently. The Thinker was the name of the chess program that all seven players would compete against. At every meet so far, a picture of Rodin's famous statue of a man thinking, chin in hand, had been prominently displayed. Lately Frank had been seeing the statue in his dreams.

"All of you won your local competitions, so I'm sure you understand the rules," Ms. Lassen continued. "But let me refresh your memories. We don't want anyone to be disqualified."

Frank realized suddenly that though the other competitors' eyes were on Ms. Lassen, their minds were probably already focused on the game. All the terminals were connected to the minicomputer set up in the middle of the playing area. It seemed amazing to Frank that one of the players sitting there would go home in three days with ten thousand dollars.

Ms. Lassen said, "As you know, this tournament is open only to amateur players, ages thirteen to nineteen. Remember that you will be playing not against one another but against the computer. This drastically increases the difficulty of the game. To beat the computer at chess, the player needs total concentration and a *very* creative mind."

"Not so creative," objected a young man a couple of seats to Frank's right. "The computer's only as good as the programmer, right? If the program has bugs, the computer can make all kinds of mistakes, thinking they're appropriate moves."

Frank craned his neck to get a look at the speaker. He was short, with black hair and big glasses. Joe, Frank thought, would have called him a nerd, but Frank considered him an intelligent opponent.

Ms. Lassen smiled tightly at the young man as if he were the village idiot. "My company has written the finest chess program in the world," she said emphatically. "Our program does not have bugs."

"Every program has bugs," the young man said, but Ms. Lassen ignored him and went on with her orientation speech. Frank heard a girl to his right laugh softly.

"Each of you will play eight games over two days. You have up to six hours a day in which to play, and we suggest you take your time. The person who wins the greatest number of games wins the tournament. In the event of a tie, the tied players will play as many games as necessary to break the tie.

"Remember, there will be no conversation of any kind once play has begun. We suggest you take the time now to mingle. We'll reconvene here at noon for the first day's play. Good luck, and may the best chess player win."

As Ms. Lassen left, the teenagers turned to one another shyly. "I guess we should introduce ourselves," Frank said as they all stood up and gathered awkwardly together. "My name is Frank Hardy. I'm the Northeastern District winner."

A bright-faced girl with long red hair extended a hand. Frank shook it. "Carlene Dunn, Miles City, Montana. Great Plains District."

A tall, dark-skinned youth with a wild, wiry haircut stepped forward to shake Frank's hand. "We've already met, Frank. Well, sort of. I'm Kyle Payton, Atlanta, Georgia. Remember?"

"Kyle!" Frank said, brightening. "I don't believe it! Sure I remember you. We used to play chess by mail when we were . . . what? Thirteen?"

"Twelve for me. My birthday's at the end of the year. Hey, good luck, man, and it's great to finally meet you in person."

"Yeah, you, too," Frank said. He knew from experience that Kyle would be a tough competitor. "Good luck."

Frank turned to shake hands with the next young man and found himself facing a player with the rugged good looks of a movie star. "I'm Victor Julian," the dark-haired boy said as Frank took in the cool, brooding eyes that made him think Victor would be tough to beat. Victor's smile was so big and infectious, however, that Frank immediately thought of him as a friend. "You look too old to be in this contest," Frank said.

Victor threw back his head and laughed. "I know, I know!" he said in an engagingly cheerful manner. "But I'm only nineteen, so I just made it under the wire. I'm from Cupertino, California. I won the Western District."

"Wow," said the girl next to Victor. Frank realized that she was only about five feet tall, and was probably much younger than the other contestants. "Cupertino's right in the heart of Silicon Valley, isn't it? I bet you know everything there is to know about computers."

Victor blushed. "Well, I try. You are . . . ?"

The girl giggled nervously. Frank smiled at how shy she was. "Oh! I'm sorry! Louisa Shan. I'm the first member of my family to be born here in the United States, which I guess means I could be president ha-ha. Um—I'm fourteen, and I come from Port Lavaca, Texas. I'm the Southwestern District champion."

"It's great meeting you," Victor said, shaking her hand.

"Jeez, talk, talk, talk," said the loud young man who had questioned Ms. Lassen. "I came here to play chess, not socialize."

"Got a name, sport?" Victor asked, turning toward him.

The young man sighed. "Name: Mike Ayres. Age: seventeen. Rank: freshman at University of Wisconsin, winner of the Great Lakes District." His rigid expression broke as he added, "I creamed those amateurs, and I'm going to kick your— Well, you know. Anyone got any other bright questions?"

Frank barely restrained a laugh. Despite the obnoxious speech and nasal voice, there was something refreshing about Mike that broke the polite tension in the room. Carlene began to chuckle, Kyle choked on his own repressed laughter, and in seconds everyone, including Mike, was laughing.

Victor looked around the room. "Where's that other guy?"

"George?" Mike asked. "George Potrero. Odd guy. I talked with him a little on the way in. He comes from the Northwest District, and he doesn't want anything to do with anyone else." Mike leaned forward and whispered conspiratorially. "I think he's sweet on some girl out here." He stressed the word *girl,* and winked as if a great secret had been passed around.

"How about a midmorning snack?" Carlene

55

said. "Our meals in the hotel coffee shop are free, you know—compliments of Rightway Electronics."

"Sounds great," Frank said, and the others nodded their agreement. Together they walked out of the auditorium, each wishing the others the best of luck, but with their fingers crossed for luck for themselves.

As Frank passed through the door, a hand plucked at his sleeve. Joe was standing there, solemnly holding a briefcase. "What are you doing here?" Frank asked. "I thought you were with Sergeant Hirsch."

"We have a little situation here, Frank. I need you to go to the bank with me."

"The—" Frank could see Joe was in no mood to explain while standing in the hotel lobby. He called to the others, "I'm going to have to skip the snack. Something's come up. I'll see you at the tournament, okay?"

His fellow chess players waved goodbye, and Frank turned back to Joe. "This had better not take too long."

"It won't," Joe said. "It's the bank here in the hotel where you went for money yesterday."

"That small branch office?" Frank asked, dismayed. When Joe nodded, he shrugged and said, "Let's go."

As Frank walked through the long hotel lobby with Joe, he had a feeling they were being watched by men lounging along the walls or playing the slot machines. The men all seemed normal enough, but there was something familiar about them—something that Frank couldn't quite put his finger on.

Then he had it. Cops. Cops were watching them.

"Here's the bank," Frank announced to his brother, feeling as nervous now as Joe was acting. He led Joe inside, where Joe steered him to the manager's desk.

The manager was a heavyset older man with pale skin and half-closed eyes. "May I help you?" he asked wearily.

"Yes," Joe said. "We need to open a savings account. A joint account for Frank and Joe Hardy."

"What?" Frank said, turning to his brother.

"I'll explain later," Joe whispered.

"How much do you wish to deposit?" the bank manager asked, pulling out a new account form and beginning to fill it out.

"This," Joe said.

The manager sat straight up in his chair as Joe opened the briefcase. Frank straightened, too, and his eyes widened when he saw the amount written on the check.

"It's a certified check," Joe pointed out, "so it should clear right away."

Frank stared at his brother, suddenly finding it impossible to breathe. "A million dollars!" he croaked as the manager examined the check suspiciously. "Joe, that's not our money."

"Shh!" Joe said. He stood up and motioned Frank to move a short distance away from the manager, who was even more suspicious after Frank's reaction.

"I told you I'd explain later," Joe muttered to his brother. "Cornelius gave it to me for the kidnappers. They insisted that *we* open a savings account and said they would withdraw the ransom later."

Frank took a step back, staring at Joe in amazement. "That's pretty dumb. How will they get money out of our account?"

Joe just shrugged.

"Do you realize," Frank said slowly, thinking, "that someone might be trying to frame us! If anything happens to that money while it's in our names, we're dead meat!"

Chapter

7

"THIS IS NOT a good day," Joe said quietly. "I honestly can't figure out what's going on."

"Me neither," Frank agreed. "This whole thing stinks. Think about it. Why us?"

"We did try to stop them. This could be some kind of payback."

"Payback, how?" Frank dismissed that suggestion with a wave. "And how do they know our names? Our names didn't enter into this until after we were picked up by the police."

"Yeah. Well, that's when all this trouble with Cornelius began, too," Joe agreed. "You don't think a cop could be behind this?"

"We can't eliminate any possibility yet," Frank said. "There's more that doesn't make sense, too. The only people who knew we were in that neon graveyard were the kidnappers. I'd assumed that that chauffeur called the cops when I took off with his car, and that the cops happened to find us by accident. But that doesn't really work. What if the kidnappers called the cops? Maybe they panicked when we got caught in that sign and called the cops to rescue us."

"Okay, here's the scenario, then," said Joe. "The kidnappers grab Beth at the airport. We chase them, but they give us the slip after we crash into that sign. They know that if we get killed while chasing them during a kidnapping they can be accused of murder. They don't want a charge like that hanging over them on top of everything else. So they report our location to the police, hoping the cops will rescue us. Hirsch takes us to the station, and when Cornelius hears about us, he figures we're in on the kidnapping. When the real kidnappers learn that Cornelius thinks we're guilty, they decide to keep us in the game to confuse things."

"*I'm* sure confused," Frank admitted. "But that brings up another interesting question. Why would the kidnappers contact the *police* about the ransom? A kidnapper always contacts the person who'll pay the money and demands that the authorities be kept out of it."

Joe shrugged. "Face it, they're either brilliant or rank amateurs. Maybe both."

"This is getting us nowhere," Frank said, exasperated. "We don't know why the kidnappers chose this bank or how they plan to get the money out of our account. *If* they plan to. Even if the bank did agree to hand over the million, they'd have to show up to accept it, and they'd be arrested.''

"Shhh.'' Joe pointed to the bank manager, who was motioning to them to return to his desk. His expression seemed more relaxed, Joe noticed, but it was still a long way from friendly.

"Here you are,'' he said in a clipped voice, sliding papers across the desk for Frank and Joe to sign. Surprised and very reluctant, Joe signed them and passed them to Frank. When Frank had signed, the manager gave the boys their copies and began stacking his own papers. "You understand, I hope, that this money will not be available for withdrawal until the check clears,'' he said.

"It's a certified check,'' Joe pointed out. "Aren't those cleared right away?''

"Not under these, um, circumstances,'' the manager replied sternly. "Don't worry, though,'' he added. "I'll telephone you personally when the proper procedures have been carried out.''

"You do that,'' Joe said, trying to sound rich. He and Frank left the man sliding down farther and farther in his chair.

"Papers,'' Hirsch said, stepping in front of Frank and Joe the second they left the bank. The boys handed over the paperwork, including the slip with their account number on it. Hirsch checked his watch—eleven-fifty.

"Isn't it about time for your game?" he asked Frank.

"Just about," Frank said uncertainly, "but what about this? What's the plan?"

"We wait," Hirsch said simply. "Just as the kidnappers demanded. Don't worry. We're keeping an eye on that money." He gave the boys a mock salute. "Keep in touch."

"I still don't like it," Joe muttered as he walked Frank back to the auditorium.

This time Frank noticed that the cops had all cleared out.

"It sure did feel like a setup to me," Joe added, "especially at the end. If I could just figure out what the angle is."

"Don't talk about it now," Frank said shortly. "I have to play chess in less than ten minutes. I can't let anything break my concentration."

"You're right. Sorry." Joe opened the auditorium door for his brother. "Knock 'em dead, Frank. I'll drop in to watch later."

"Thanks. What are you going to do in the meantime?"

"I thought I'd take a look around town."

"Yeah, there's a lot to see," Frank said.

"Like Beth's fiancé, maybe," Joe agreed. "It won't be easy to find him, since I don't know his name, but Beth said he worked at one of the hotels around here."

62

"Good idea," said Frank. "Watch yourself."

"By the way," said Joe, "did you memorize our account number?"

Frank smiled. "Of course." He went into the auditorium.

Joe decided to check out the personnel at the hotels along the Strip first, hoping to get lucky and find Beth's fiancé. That is, he reminded himself, if there is a fiancé. But if there isn't, why would Beth make the story up? He shook his head. The more he tried to figure out this case, the more complicated it got. He decided to have a talk with the clerks at his own hotel before trying the other establishments. "Who knows?" he said, talking to himself as he crossed the huge lobby. "The way things have been happening this weekend, I might run into Beth and her kidnappers in one of the casinos here. If I did, I wouldn't be at all surprised." Joe noticed people staring at him and promised not to talk to himself anymore.

A friendly talk with the desk clerk convinced Joe that no young male employees were missing any wealthy girlfriends due in from New York. Disappointed but still optimistic, Joe left the hotel and headed for another hotel complex shaped like an enormous spouting whale.

It was so hot and bright outside that Joe could understand why few people ever walked anyplace. One other guy on the street forced Joe to do a double take, though. It took him a couple of seconds to realize the man was just an Elvis Presley impersonator—not the real thing.

Joe took a shortcut across the whale hotel's parking lot, and his heart skipped a beat when he spotted a sedan that resembled the dusty yellow car. Unable to resist, Joe walked around the back to check the license plate. Then he remembered he had never memorized the number. Joe pressed his face against a side window and peered inside. There was nothing unusual in the car. It was obviously just a look-alike car.

Joe was about to turn to go when he caught a glimpse of movement behind him reflected in the window. Surprised, Joe wheeled around—just quickly enough to see a mustached face behind him.

Then something cracked against the top of his skull, and Joe pitched forward without a word and landed against the yellow car.

Frank left the auditorium in an even worse mood than when he'd entered it. Of the four games of the day, he had won only two. No big surprise, he told himself. My concentration's shot.

"Not a good day, Frankie boy?" Mike Ayres remarked, barely suppressing his gloating as he followed Frank out the doors. All around them, spectators were still milling, staring curiously at the boys and pointing them out to their friends. "How many games are you up now?"

Frank told him. "And you?"

"Four. I won all of them," Mike said proudly. "You guys might as well pack it in and go home. This baby is mine."

"There's always tomorrow," Victor pointed out, joining them outside the auditorium doors.

"Yeah, right." Mike walked away, laughing.

Frank turned to the older boy with relief as they walked away from the crowd. "How did you do?" Frank asked him.

"Three," Victor admitted, not quite able to conceal his satisfaction. "But I bet you're just warming up, right?"

"I've got a lot on my mind," Frank said feebly.

"Oh, yeah?" Victor sounded fascinated. "Like what?"

Frank started to answer, but just then his attention was drawn to a wiry, grim-faced teenager pushing past them. The kid kept his head down and continually swiped at his nose with a wadded-up tissue. Frank noticed the tension in his hunched-up shoulders. "There's George Potrero," Frank said. "Think we should go after him and try to talk?"

Victor seemed to be uninterested. "He looks as if he wants to be left alone. Speaking of which, I've got stuff to take care of myself. See you tomorrow, pal." With a slap on the back—

a little too hard, Frank thought—Victor started for the elevators.

Frank was left alone, wondering where Joe was. He was exhausted by the long, disappointing meet and really wanted to talk to Joe. He had expected him to show up by now. I hope he didn't get into trouble, Frank thought, starting to worry.

Frank's thoughts were interrupted when a short, round man in a tuxedo and a younger, taller, gloomy-looking man in a white dinner jacket appeared in front of him. "Frank Hardy?" the short man asked in a high-pitched voice, causing his several chins to wiggle. Frank noticed that the man's nose must have been broken at one time and set badly. It was a little crooked, pointing from his right eyebrow to the left corner of his mouth. "May we have a moment of your time?"

"I guess so," Frank said, glancing at the taller man, who peered down at Frank with what appeared to be a dimly lit brain.

"In private, of course," the fat man said. Before Frank could answer, the men grabbed both of his arms and hustled him down the hall and through a door.

"Hey, wait a minute," Frank said, recovering slowly. By the time he realized he was being forced out of the hotel, he found himself in a back alley with the two goons, next to a Dumpster.

"What's going on here?" Frank demanded. "Who are you guys?"

"Call me Iggy," said the fat man with such dignity that Frank wanted to laugh. "And this is Mose."

"Iggy?" Frank said, stalling for time. "You mean there really are people named Iggy?"

Iggy looked hurt. "Do I make fun of your name?" Then his face brightened, as if he had thought of a joke for the first time in his life. "Uh, listen, Hardy, can I be frank? Get it— *Frank?*"

"Oh, brother," Frank groaned.

Iggy smiled, and his eyes became slits, lost in rounds of fleshy cheeks. "Well! Enough chit-chat," he said briskly. "A close friend tipped us off to the possibility of becoming partners with you in your chess venture. We were hoping to discuss business with you today, but I'm afraid you let us down this afternoon."

"Excuse me?" said Frank.

"I'll explain," Iggy said. "Mose here and I wagered a very large sum of money on your winning this tournament. Our faith in your talent and intelligence convinced us to risk our finances on you, despite the long odds against you."

"Long odds?" Frank said, confused. "You mean, everyone figures I'll lose?"

Iggy nodded his head sadly.

"I can't believe you bet on chess tournaments," Frank said, running a hand through his hair. "You must be professional gamblers."

"Me and Mose prefer the term 'probability speculators,' " Iggy said, correcting him. Mose blinked sleepily and nodded. "Our close friend told us you had an inside track to win. He also assured us you had a brother whose personal safety was important to you."

Joe, Frank thought. "What did you do with Joe?" He curled a fist.

Mose, suddenly alert, stepped toward him.

"No violence, please," Iggy said. "We haven't seen your brother, but our friend knows where to find him."

"This friend—would he be Jerome Cornelius?"

From the expression on Iggy's face, Frank could tell he had hit a nerve. Iggy had definitely heard the name before. Cornelius must have put the two gamblers up to this.

Iggy composed himself. "Let us leave names out of this. Do you understand the meaning of this conversation?"

"Oh, sure, I get it," said Frank. "You want me to win, or else—what? Something may happen to Joe?"

"I'm afraid you still don't comprehend how important this is," Iggy said. He snapped his fingers. Mose moved like lightning, slamming a hammer of a fist into Frank's stomach. Frank gasped and sank weakly to his knees.

"Now perhaps you understand," Iggy said,

standing over him. "We want you to try your best tomorrow. No more stupid mistakes, eh, Frank? Concentration is everything in chess. We're counting on you."

His stomach aching, Frank got to his feet after they had disappeared. For a moment he thought about what he'd like to do to Cornelius.

Soon, though, he went back to worrying about what had happened to Joe.

Water splashed against Joe's face and woke him up. When he opened his eyes it was still pitch dark.

Where am I? he wondered groggily, trying to sit up. His arms and legs were stiff. He wiggled his hands, pleased that his wrists weren't tied. He wondered what he was lying on and why he was in such an uncomfortable position.

He tried again to straighten up and this time smacked his head against metal. He felt the cold steel against the top of his head as water seeped up around his legs and hips. What is this place? he asked himself, starting to panic. How did I get here? He tried to remember the last thing that had happened. He had a vague memory of standing outside a yellow car, glimpsing a mustached man behind him. Then there was nothing.

Could the man have knocked me unconscious? Joe wondered. With a sense of dread he realized that was what had happened.

Joe's knee collided with something hard that

gave slightly under the impact. He groped frantically for the object, and realized it was a tire.

I'm in a car trunk! he knew all at once. And it's filling with water. The car must be sinking in water. Someone is trying to kill me!

"Help!" Joe yelled, beating against the top of the trunk. He knew it was hopeless because it was unlikely that anyone would be around to hear him. I'm going to drown!

No one came to help him, and panic rushed over Joe as the water gushed in to drive out the last of his air.

Chapter

8

JOE SHOVED HIS FACE into the uppermost corner of the trunk and gulped in the last pocket of air before the rising water pushed it out, too. Holding his breath, he kicked at the trunk lid, but it didn't give.

Trapped! The word rang in his head like a bell tolling.

Unable to see in the pitch dark, Joe felt around the trunk. It held nothing else but the spare tire.

A spare tire was something no one would have thought to take out of a trunk, but it was all Joe needed. As his lungs began to burn, he released the brace that held the tire to the bottom of the trunk. Pressing his back against the hood, he lifted the tire off its mount. Water rushed in under the rubber tire, pushing it up.

Joe felt around on the trunk floor where the tire had been mounted, and found what he needed.

In his hands were tools for changing a tire. Joe held on to the tire iron and threw the other tools aside.

Ignoring the spots swimming in front of his eyes, Joe allowed the last bit of useless air to explode from his lungs. His heart pounding, he used his last ounce of strength to jam the sharp-ended tire iron into the tire, near the rim where the rubber was weakest. A large bubble of air burst from where Joe had popped the inner tube.

Joe capped his lips around the hole as tightly as possible to seal out the water. Foul-tasting, oily air rushed into his mouth, and he fought the urge to gag and spit it out.

Holding as much air in his lungs as he could, Joe now forced the tire iron under the trunk latch and pushed down with all his weight. The latch held, and he worried that he wouldn't have the energy to budge it. If not now, never, he told himself, feeling his lungs working to expel the old air again. The latch continued to hold firm. He twisted for a better position, getting his chest above the tire iron. Gripping the tire iron beneath his chest with both hands, Joe forced his weight down on the bar.

The latch creaked and wobbled, but the bar had rammed into his ribs, and Joe spat in pain. The air rushed out of him.

But the latch finally gave. The trunk popped up.

Joe shot up out of the trunk, and an instant later broke through the surface of the water. He was in a pond or lake, he dimly realized as he floated, gasping for air. Somewhere far away were lights, blurred by the water in his eyes. Then he stopped thinking and relied on instinct to lead him toward the lights.

When Joe woke up, he couldn't be sure how long he had been lying on the shore. It was night, and the air was chilly. He was shivering in his wet clothes. Now that he was able to breathe, he knelt to sip water from the lake and rinse the taste of tire rubber from his mouth.

He looked around, his eyes adjusting to the moonlit darkness. Behind him, in the distance, there were mountains. Just behind him was a dirt path that ran from the lake into a mass of large fir trees. The lake seemed to go on forever.

He thought back, remembering the yellow car. The face with the mustache. Joe realized now that it was the face of the burly kidnapper who had shoved Beth into the car. Of course, Joe realized, the yellow sedan he'd seen probably wasn't the same car in which Beth had been carried away. But it might be the car that lay at the bottom of the lake now. Joe hoped he could tell the police where this lake was so they could dredge it up.

Are they done with me now? Joe wondered.

Did they dump me because I served my purpose when I deposited that money in the bank? And if they're done with me, what about Frank? Joe couldn't figure it out. Only he and his brother had the authority to withdraw the ransom money. Or was there some reason why the kidnappers might want the money to stay in the bank?

One thing Joe knew for sure. He was never going to figure it out if he froze to death where he was.

He stood and stretched his cramped muscles. Water dripped from his soggy clothes. Clapping his hands on his arms to warm himself, Joe started along the lakeshore path.

He spotted the old dirt road before he saw the clearing among the trees. Small log cabins dotted the clearing. In two of them lights flickered, and smoke drifted from their stone chimneys. The other cabins appeared unoccupied. Frank saw no wires to indicate that any of them had electricity or telephones, but he hoped one of them had a car or a radio transmitter.

Joe approached the nearest cabin just as a woman came out. She looked old and frail, and she wore a tattered sweater over a shapeless housedress. The old woman was collecting logs from a woodpile around the side of the cabin when she saw Joe on the path. She instantly froze with fear.

"You stay away from me!" the old woman

shouted, waving a stick of firewood in front of her like a club. Wide-eyed, she backed toward the cabin as quickly as she could, never taking her eyes off Joe.

"I need some—" Joe began. Before he could continue, the old woman reached the cabin, hurried in, and slammed the door. Joe heard a bolt slipping into place inside.

"Hey!" he yelled, pressing his face close to a cabin window. The old woman was nowhere to be seen. As Joe backed away, the window mirrored his face back at him. He jumped when he realized what he had seen.

No wonder I scared her, he thought. His clothes were wet and stained, his hair matted, and his face smeared with mud. A black smudge marred his left cheek to the corner of his mouth.

Gee, I look like a demented clown. Joe knew there was no way the old woman was going to let him into her isolated home.

Joe washed his face in the lake and straightened his hair as best as he could. He passed several of the darkened cabins, but, as he expected, no one was home and there were no telephones in sight. He passed a sign that read Lake Mead Cabins. Joe knew where he was at last. Lake Mead was about twenty miles east of Las Vegas, he told himself with satisfaction.

Encouraged by the knowledge, Joe jogged toward the only other occupied cabin. He wanted to get close enough to be able to speak before he was seen. As he neared the cabin, he heard heavy metal music. It sounded distant and tinny, as though it was coming from a cheap radio.

Joe was encouraged. The music meant some-one around his age might be in the cabin. He pounded on the door.

A pretty blond girl opened the door. In the flicker of candlelight from inside the cabin, Joe could barely make out the features of her face. He did see her eyes widen and her jaw drop, though.

She stepped back to reveal the horror in her face and said, "Joe Hardy?"

Joe gaped. He knew the voice, but he couldn't believe who it was. "Beth?"

Her only answer was the terrified sweep of her arm. The portable radio in her hand slammed against the side of his head, and Joe toppled backward into the night.

Chapter

9

FRANK SAT in the hotel coffee shop, studying the menu. The menu was shaped like a tiny harp and featured items such as the Sir Lancelotta-burger and Sirloin the Magician. The salt and pepper shakers were pewter stallions in full battle armor. Frank ordered a Sir Galasalad and wondered why everything in this town had to be cute.

Frank was getting tired of Las Vegas.

"Frank!"

He forced himself to smile and wave at Victor, who was striding toward him as if he considered Frank his best friend. Frank was happy to see Victor, but he wished it were Joe instead. Frank hadn't heard from his brother since the tournament began, and it was now nearly eight o'clock.

77

Frank knew his anxiety showed, because the minute Victor sat down, he said, "Hey, man, what's wrong?"

"Family stuff," Frank said, shrugging off the question. "My brother's supposed to be here, but he's out doing the town, I guess."

"That's family for you," Victor said, waving cheerfully across the room to Louisa and Carlene, who were eating omelets several tables away. "Never around when you need them."

"You have problems with your family?" Frank asked, making conversation.

Victor returned his gaze to Frank. "I don't even have a family," Victor said abruptly. "A real one, I mean. I'm an only child, and adopted. Actually, I heard a rumor my real mother and a sister live in Pennsylvania somewhere, but I haven't gotten around to checking it out."

"Adopted?" Victor's cheerful coldness struck Frank as odd. Frank knew several adopted kids, and he'd never known them to claim that their adoptive family wasn't a real family. And if those kids knew where their biological parents might be, they'd check it out right away.

"Yeah," said Victor, taking Frank's menu and scanning it. "I guess that's why I picked up on chess. It was something reliable to hold on to."

"It must be tough," Frank said. He still sensed something fishy, but his attention lapsed.

He hardly knew Victor, after all, and that night his mind was on his brother.

"It hasn't been so bad." Victor flashed Frank a conspiratorial wink. "At lease I've always had girlfriends. You have a girlfriend, Frank?"

Frank, surprised at the change of subject, took out his wallet. He was proud of his girlfriend, Callie, and loved to show her picture to anyone. He flipped the wallet open to a photo in a plastic sleeve.

"Callie Shaw," Frank said, showing the photo to Victor, who let out a soft, slow whistle.

"She's a knockout," Victor said. His eyes flickered up to the coffee shop entrance. His expression changed as he stood and waved.

"Hey, George! over here," Victor called, causing several diners to notice him and then keep staring admiringly. Watching his impact on the women in the dining area, Frank wondered why they weren't crowding around the handsome chess player this very minute.

From the doorway George Potrero gave Victor a curt nod as the hostess whisked him to the opposite side of the coffee shop, out of sight of Victor and Frank.

"He's a weird guy, that George," Victor said, sitting down. "Antisocial, you know? He won't talk to anyone but Mike, and I think he talks to him out of self-defense. You know how much Mike talks." Victor leaned across the table, lowering his voice to a whisper. "Mike said George is mad all the time because he was all set to marry his girlfriend before her father made them call it off."

Frank cocked an eyebrow. "Go on."

"That's about it," Victor said. "Word is that's what George is doing in town—trying to win the prize money to prove to her old man he can hack it as a money-maker."

Frank wondered silently if the rumor was true. It seemed farfetched to think Potrero might be Beth's missing fiancé, but still, it was the only lead he'd come across so far.

Victor grinned and pulled up closer to the table. "Hey, Frank. We ought to play detective, huh? We could tail him and figure out what his secret is. There'd be a way to pass the time between chess games!"

Frank froze, wondering just how much Victor knew about him. "You watch too much television," Frank said casually. The waitress brought his salad. "Ordering anything?"

Victor shook his head. "I've got a date, sort of," he said with a smile. "I promised I'd visit some friends of my adoptive parents while I was in Las Vegas."

"Have fun," Frank said. Victor got up, and Frank realized he was glad to be rid of him. Frank wanted to think about George Potrero. Maybe he and Joe could check out Potrero and the other chess players.

Where, he wondered, could Joe be?

A few minutes later Frank had finished his salad, paid the bill at the checkout counter, and bought a newspaper. On his way out, Frank had stolen a quick glance around the coffee shop. George was still there, eating alone. After nearly every bite, he was forced to stop and wipe his nose on a wad of tissues. With a cold like that, no wonder he keeps to himself, Frank thought.

Frank found a bench within sight of the coffee shop entrance and sat down. He opened his paper and pretended to read it slowly. Every few seconds he peeked over at the coffee shop, watching for George.

Frank sat there for half an hour, flipping through the same pages over and over, reading nothing. He wondered how anyone eating by himself could spend so much time on a meal. It was as if George had a reason not to leave the restaurant.

At last he did come out and walked toward Frank. Frank held up his paper, hoping to hide his face. George marched past. As far as Frank could tell, George hadn't seen him.

Frank counted to ten, dropped the paper on the bench, and started out after George.

The dour-faced youth walked through the hotel lobby, past the slot machines where tourists shoved coin after coin into the one-armed bandits, and out the front door, clutching tissues in one hand.

Frank followed him outside and for a moment

was stunned by the colors and lights that greeted him on the Strip. He'd been so preoccupied—first with the tournament, then with the kidnapping, then with Joe's disappearance—that he'd forgotten that Las Vegas was just outside the hotel's front door. Wherever he looked there were flashing signs and sparkling lights, and from every door came the constant clanging of slot machines and other games.

Frank saw George hurrying down the Strip to hail a cab. Frank ran after him and made it to the street just as a cab pulled up to the curb. "George!" Frank yelled, waving to get his attention.

George ignored him, reaching for the door handle instead.

"George Potrero! Wait a minute!" Frustrated at being ignored, Frank ran up to the boy and grabbed him by the shoulder.

Potrero pulled away and spun around to face Frank. His eyes were wide, and he wore a panic-stricken expression. Without a word he climbed into the cab. As the taxi drove away, Frank tried to wave down a second one.

To his surprise a station wagon pulled up beside him instead. The back door popped open.

"How nice to see you again, Frank. Please. Get in."

Frank groaned. It was Iggy.

Iggy leaned out the door, opening his jacket

just enough for Frank to see a pistol in a shoulder holster.

"If you please," Iggy said. "There has been a change in our situation, and we must discuss it with you."

Frank rolled his eyes and climbed in.

"Hey, Mose," he said to the driver. Mose grunted a reply and pulled the station wagon out into traffic.

"To the north," Iggy told Mose. He turned to face Frank. "An interesting situation has come up, Frank, and you could be very helpful to us."

"Do tell," Frank said, humoring the gambler.

"It seems that our acquaintance has changed the odds on you somewhat."

"Cornelius?" Frank asked. Suddenly he was interested. "Now he's an acquaintance? I thought he was our 'mutual friend.' What did he do?"

Iggy frowned, then continued. "This person has placed a very sizable bet on you. Naturally this has changed the odds considerably. You are now an even two-to-one."

"Oh," Frank said. "So, let's see, all of the people who bet on me will win two dollars for every dollar they bet—*if* I win, right?" He shook his head, chuckling. "I still can't believe you guys bet on chess," Frank said. "Anyway, that's good news, right? Didn't you bet on me to win?"

Iggy grimaced. "The odds on you used to be

five-to-one. The profits on two-to-one odds are obviously less than the returns on five-to-one odds. Instead of winning five dollars for every dollar we bet, we'd now win only two. As a result, Mose and me have been forced to change our wager."

Frank stared at him. "You're betting more on me?"

"We are betting against you," Iggy replied sullenly.

Frank could barely keep from laughing. "So what do you want me to do? Throw the tournament?"

Iggy was dead silent. Frank stared, no longer finding the situation funny.

"You do want me to throw the tournament! I won't do it!"

Iggy sighed and spoke to Mose. "Frank has decided to be difficult, Mose. You know where to go." To Frank he said, "The three of us would appreciate the pleasure of your company."

"Three—"

Iggy pulled his jacket open again, flashing the pistol at Frank.

Frank sank deeper into his seat, wishing he had never learned to play chess.

"Out," Iggy commanded in his high voice. Frank knew they were in the desert somewhere north of Las Vegas, but they had left the main road long ago. The station wagon had traveled for close to two hours, and while much of that was on winding back roads, Frank calculated he was at least eighty miles from town.

Iggy reached across the back seat and unlatched Frank's door. Then he shoved Frank out of the car.

Hardly believing what the two guys were up to, Frank watched Iggy come around to his side, pistol drawn. "You're not going to shoot me," Frank said uncertainly.

"No," Iggy said. "We are discussing money in the range of seven figures, but we do not normally shoot people over money. No, making you disappear for a time will suit our purposes just fine."

"In other words," Frank said, "if I'm not there, I forfeit and I lose."

"You're a smart boy," Iggy said. "Take off your clothes."

"What?" said Frank.

Iggy fired a shot into the ground at Frank's feet. Without another word Frank peeled off his shirt, shoes, and slacks. Mose collected the clothes as they fell to the desert floor.

Wrapping his arms around himself, Frank sullenly watched Mose gather them. "I could die out here in just my underwear," he said.

"Only of embarrassment." Iggy got into the car and looked back out the window at Frank. "Thank you for your cooperation," he said.

"Watch out for scorpions and reptiles. They like the desert at this time of year."

With a screech, the car sped off. Frank ran after it until the taillights faded into the distance.

The silence of the desert swallowed him. He was alone. Is it my imagination, he asked himself, peering around nervously in the moonlight, or do I hear a snake's rattle?

Chapter

10

"THEY WON'T BITE ME if I don't bother them. They won't bite me if I don't bother them," Frank chanted aloud as he jogged through the desert, ignoring the pain in his feet. He had long since stopped paying attention to the pebbles that stung his toes and the grains of sand that cut like tiny bits of glass. He jogged because, without clothes, moving quickly was the only way to keep himself warm.

Besides, it helped distract him from the thing he hated most—snakes hiding in the dark, waiting to strike at him.

Frank calculated he had gone about four miles in the hour since Mose and Iggy had left him. He thought about the tournament, but drove it from his mind. He had more important things to think about now. He had yet to find a road, for example. He was making his way south by reading the stars that shone brightly over the desert, but he had no way of knowing where Las Vegas was. As cold as the desert night was, the day would be even hotter. He wondered how long it would be before he could relax by the hotel pool and enjoy a tall iced soda.

As he ran, Frank scanned the desert for signs of civilization. A shack, a road, a light. So far, nothing.

Finally he stopped, panting. The instant he stood still, his legs turned to rubber and he sank to his knees.

At least there are no scorpions, Frank thought. The snake he thought he'd heard had never materialized. Of course he'd run into more than one cactus in the past few hours. Wondering for the thousandth time what had become of Joe, Frank shivered as a cold breeze whipped across the desert.

"Get up!" Frank yelled to himself. Slowly he got to his feet. "Now make a fire," he said out loud to hear himself talk. He imagined that someone might see the flames and come looking for him, but he knew the fire's only real value would be to keep warm.

Frank moved quickly around the desert, gathering bits of brush until he had a small pile of it. It took longer to find the rocks he needed. At last he had two that would give off sparks when struck together.

On his third try Frank set the brush on fire. He crouched next to it, warming himself, suddenly feeling very hungry and wishing he'd had more than a salad for dinner.

The wind blew up again, but Frank ignored it. He closed his eyes, soaking up the heat, and didn't notice as bits of brush blew off the fire, carrying sparks across the desert floor.

Gradually Frank became aware of the heat at his back as well. His eyes snapped open, and he spun around.

At first the entire desert seemed to be on fire. Then Frank realized that a clump of burning tumbleweed had blown into a dried-up old acacia tree. Because the wood was extremely dry, the flames caught immediately and rose up high in the wind, but Frank could see that the fire was unlikely to spread farther.

Fine, then, he thought as the flames soared higher. Two bonfires are better than one.

He glanced up at the sky and for a moment thought he was fantasizing. One of the stars moved. Then the tiny dot of light started circling around him. A beating sound grew louder, until it was pounding in his ears. Frank waved frantically, trying to signal the helicopter.

It hovered near him, then dropped to the desert. As it landed, its bright headlight hit Frank, blinding him. Dimly Frank could make out figures scrambling from the copter. As his eyes adjusted, he was shocked to see a ring of rifles surrounding him, all trained on him.

"You are trespassing on restricted United States government property," boomed a voice through a megaphone. "You're under arrest."

Joe woke in darkness again. His face itched. He tried to scratch it and found he couldn't move his hands. His wrists were tied behind him.

He tried to move his feet. They were bound, too. He was flat on his back, bouncing slightly, and when he stretched his legs, his feet hit a wall. He pushed with his toes until his head touched the opposite wall. Plastic crinkled beneath him as he moved.

Joe inhaled deeply, and rough cloth flapped in his mouth and nose.

I'm in a car, he thought, trying to stay calm. With a burlap bag over my head.

"Do you promise you won't hurt him?"

Joe recognized Beth's voice. He guessed she was sitting in the middle of the front seat, if he was stretched across the back.

"He's seen you. He can give us away." The gruff voice of an older man came from Beth's right. Joe knew now what no one else suspected—that Beth was the kidnapper's partner, not his victim.

Joe said nothing, wanting them to think he was still unconscious.

Beth said, "Why can't we keep him at the cabin, out of the way, until this thing is over?"

"The cabin's no good." This was a new voice, male and young, from the driver's seat. "If he was smart enough to figure out where we were, others will, too. We can't afford to be caught now. One more day and we'll be rich beyond our wildest dreams."

"You don't get it, do you?" the older man said. "If he's around, it'll never be over. He'll always be able to tell what he knows to the police, whether he does it now or in ten years. He'll always be a threat to us."

"Look, Burke—" the young man said. Before he could continue, the older man exploded. "Don't say that name here!" he snarled. "You don't know if that kid's still unconscious! I don't want to be identified to the cops because you have a big mouth!"

There was a long silence. Joe guessed they were looking at him, trying to tell if he was awake and listening. He stayed as still as possible.

Finally they seemed convinced that Joe was still out, because the young man continued in a softer voice. "You're the professional," he said. "That's why we brought you in on this scheme. But I agree with Beth. We can't hurt anyone, no matter what. Keep him somewhere until we

91

get the money, and then cut him loose. Once we have the money, it won't matter what he knows. We'll be long gone."

"Okay, okay," Burke replied, but to Joe he didn't sound convinced.

"This is all my fault," Beth moaned. "He was just being nice to me on the plane. We shouldn't have dragged him and his brother into this."

"They dragged themselves into it," the young man said. "Nobody asked them to try to stop the kidnapping."

"But you knew they would," Beth said. "As soon as you heard Frank Hardy had won his regional competition, you told me to get a ticket on the plane he was on. What did you call it? A gambit?"

Joe jerked his head up. He forced himself to keep his mouth closed and hoped they hadn't seen him react. How did they know about Frank? Joe wondered. He tried to remember what Frank had told him about gambits during the flight to Los Vegas. Something about sacrificing a piece to gain an advantage. Sacrificing Beth, perhaps? Joe pondered the possibilities. Were they hoping to gain an advantage over the police, perhaps, by distracting them with the Hardys while their accomplice quietly ran off with the ransom money?

"Right," the young man said. "A gambit. Anyway, just because I knew he and his brother would stick their noses in doesn't mean I made them do it. And it's lucky for us they did. They gave your father and the police someone to suspect."

"If only—" Beth began mournfully.

The young man cut her off. "If only your father wasn't a pigheaded creep, that's what you mean. He's the one who was so hot to keep us apart. Well, his money will make it possible for us to be together, no matter what he wants."

"I just wish we could break free of him some other way," Beth said.

Burke spoke up. "I hate to ruin such a romantic moment, but here's the place."

Joe felt the car roll to a stop with its engine running, and he heard two doors open. Then Joe heard other cars whizzing past and slot machines ringing. He guessed he was on a street somewhere in Las Vegas. One of the car doors slammed shut, followed a few seconds later by the driver's door.

"Promise you won't hurt him," Joe heard Beth say, her voice farther off now.

Burke's voice drifted back from the driver's seat. Only he and Joe were in the car now. "You have my word."

Joe strained at the ropes around his wrists. He could feel them loosen. He twisted his hands back and forth, slowly working on the ropes.

The car lurched into gear and began to cruise slowly.

Then Joe heard a frightening noise—a sliding

sound, followed by a sharp metallic crack. Joe had heard those sounds before. Someone was preparing a hand gun for use. Next, Joe heard the rough rasp of a large screw being threaded and turned.

Joe suspected it was a silencer.

Outside he could still hear passing traffic and honking horns. Even a silenced weapon would make a sound, but most people would ignore it. It would sound very much like a clap or a slap or a heavy book being dropped.

Suddenly Joe understood why he was lying on plastic. Burke was trying to avoid a mess on the back seat.

The ropes on his wrists held, no matter how hard he strained against them.

A cold, hollow shape the size of a quarter pressed under Joe's chin. It was the tip of the silencer.

From the front seat, Burke's voice sounded almost gentle. "This isn't going to hurt a bit."

Chapter

11

JOE BROUGHT HIS KNEES up hard, managing to knock Burke's hand into the air just as the gun went off. Joe heard the rear window shatter as the shot passed through it. Outside, someone screamed.

The car swayed, and Burke muttered angrily under his breath. He's losing control, Joe thought. It was only a matter of seconds, he knew, before Burke would fire again. This time he would be expecting a moving target.

Joe flung his head up, banging it into the door handle. The door flew open. Joe kicked against the opposite door, shoving himself halfway out of the car, but not yet landing on the pavement. With a loud clap, a bullet seared through Joe's pant leg and smacked into the seat.

Joe snaked the rest of the way out of the car and fell into the street. He rolled, catching the impact on his shoulder. Car horns blared to life as tires screeched.

He knew he had brought the traffic to a halt.

The ropes fell from his wrists as he finally wriggled free of them. Joe sat up and pulled the bag from his head. He had made it to the sidewalk and was sitting right in front of the entrance to a nightclub. Above him a giant neon cowboy tipped his hat, apparently right at Joe. Voices were shouting all around him.

"He's not dead."

"Somebody call a cop!"

"He needs an ambulance."

"This has to be some kind of stunt."

"I'm all right," Joe yelled to calm down the crowd gathering around him. He tore at the ropes around his ankles. They tangled. Joe kicked his shoes off and slipped his feet through the loosened ropes.

He grabbed up his shoes and pushed his way through the crowd. No one barred his way.

The Strip was crowded with cars. Joe looked for one with its back window blown out. He didn't see it.

Burke was gone.

At least I have a name to work with now, Joe thought. He heard a siren approaching. Quickly he slipped his shoes on and hurried to the curb, blending in with the crowd. He planned to tell

Hirsch all about Burke, the sunken car, and especially Beth, but first he had to talk to Frank.

So Beth had conspired in her own kidnapping, he told himself. Why? From what the third person had said, Frank presumed that Burke was hired to help carry out this scheme. Burke, Joe guessed, was a career criminal, a thug for hire, and a hefty cut of a million-dollar ransom was enough motivation to ensure his involvement. Without Joe, it seemed that Burke and the others had no chance to recovering the ransom. But Burke, despite his taste for brutality, hadn't seemed to Joe to be a stupid man. Yet Burke had tried to kill Joe twice that night, first by drowning him and then by shooting him. Joe had no doubt it was Burke who stuffed him in the trunk of the car at Lake Mead. But he didn't think Beth knew anything about that.

Why had Burke tried to kill him the first time, before Joe knew about Beth and her plan? And why would Burke want him dead when it meant losing the money?

Unless—Joe thought. What if they *didn't* need him to get the money?

If the money was taken from the bank, Joe knew, the police would have to blame the only people who could legally withdraw it.

The Hardys.

It all hinged, he realized, on the young man in the car. Unless there was someone else involved whom Joe was unaware of, the young man was the brains of the operation. Joe hadn't heard his name or seen his face, but he knew what the young man sounded like.

He remembered what the young man had said about getting Frank involved, possibly to give the police someone to suspect. He remembered the man talking about a gambit. Suddenly Joe knew that everything hinged on the chess tournament. The young man was involved with the competition.

The competition—that was where Joe would find the answers.

It took Joe less than fifteen minutes to walk to the Camelot. Tourists hurrying from hotel to casino hardly noticed his disheveled appearance. On the side lawn of the Camelot Joe noticed several people staring at a helicopter that had just landed, its rotors still turning and kicking up noise and dust. Joe thought for a moment about seeing what was going on, then decided against it. He'd been through enough and needed to change.

He entered the lobby and headed for the elevators. He turned the key over and over in his pocket, eager to get to his room.

"Joe!"

Joe turned to see Frank walking toward him. Frank was dressed in an oversize khaki jumpsuit and big black boots.

"Nice outfit," Joe quipped. "What's this, the

98

military look? What are you doing up at two in the morning?"

"This is Las Vegas, Joe. Everyone's up at two in the morning," said Frank. "I took a moonlight stroll in the desert."

"Frank!" Joe said with mock outrage. "What will Callie say?"

"I was alone," Frank said. "And it wasn't my idea."

"What?" Joe said, his eyes widening.

Frank told him about the gamblers, the fire, and his arrest by the U.S. Air Force.

"After they heard my story," Frank concluded, "they gave me these clothes and brought me back here. I just got off the helicopter."

"That was you?" Joe said incredulously. "Boy, no one ever gives me helicopter rides."

"Believe me, you were better off doing what you were doing," Frank said. "What *were* you doing, anyway? Where have you been? You were supposed to drop in on the competition, remember?"

"Oh, I went for a swim and then a little drive," Joe replied. "Frank, I found Beth Cornelius."

Frank grabbed Joe's arm and pulled him to one side of the lobby. Frank glanced around to make sure no one was in earshot, then whispered, "What do you mean, you found her?"

Joe recounted his evening's adventures. When he was done, Frank let out a long, low whistle.

"I knew it," Frank said. "I had a feeling he was involved."

"You know who the driver was?" Joe asked.

"I think so," replied Frank. "One of the contestants has been acting really strange. His name's George Potrero."

"Hmmm," Joe said. "Can we prove anything against him?"

Frank shook his head. "Let's keep this between us. There's no point in going to Hirsch with it until we're sure. But we do need to tell him about Burke and Beth Cornelius. I doubt that either one is going to want to risk our getting out of here now, knowing what we know."

"I know how we can be sure about this Potrero guy," Joe said. "I know his voice. Let's call his room."

"Joe, it's two in the morning."

Joe shrugged. "So he'll have to answer the phone. It's the perfect time to call. Let's go."

They went to the house phone. The house operator answered and connected Joe to George's room. The phone rang.

After six rings the operator came back on the line and asked Joe if he wanted to leave a message. Joe hung up.

"He's not here, Frank," Joe said.

"That's even more suspicious," Frank replied. He yawned and stretched his arms.

"Yeah," Joe agreed.

Suddenly Frank grabbed Joe's arm and yanked him behind a timber pillar.

"What's going on?" Joe said.

"Look over there," Frank said, pointing. Joe did and noticed two men, a round little man in an expensive suit and a tall, morose-looking man. "That's Iggy and Mose."

"The gamblers?" Joe said. "Let's get them."

"No," said Frank. "I'd rather they didn't know I'm back. They might think of other ways to occupy my time for me."

The Hardys hurried toward the elevators. Before they could reach them, though, the doors of Camelot's concert hall swung open and people wandered out, blocking their way.

Joe groaned. Out of the concert hall came a grim-looking Jerome Cornelius and his henchman, Elroy. "I don't think they saw us, Frank," he said. "This way."

They ducked down another corridor, away from the concertgoers.

"This is a dead end," Frank said. "It only goes into the auditorium where the chess tournament is being held."

"Good," Joe said. "Then no one's likely to come this way."

Frank's eyes opened very wide. He studied the darkened, deserted corridor. "Joe, something's wrong. There's supposed to be a security man guarding this door. Where is he?"

No one was there. Cautiously Frank neared

the auditorium door. He tried the knob. It turned, but the door didn't open.

He threw his weight against the door, and it gave slightly. "Something's jamming it from the inside," Frank said. Joe helped push. They opened it far enough so Frank could get his hand in. He felt for whatever was blocking the door.

Frank's hand hit a large fleshy lump. "It's the guard," he said.

Once inside, Joe felt for a pulse and found one. He could smell chloroform on the man's face.

Frank scanned the room, his eyes adjusting to the darkness. Everything seemed normal. Everything but the silhouette that gradually took shape crouching in front of the mini-mainframe, apparently working on it.

"Joe!" Frank whispered. "Someone's sabotaging the computer!"

Chapter

12

FRANK FOUND THE SWITCHES near the door and flicked them on. The room exploded with bright white light.

The figure on the stage, at the computer, had flung an arm over his face, to prevent Frank and Joe from seeing who he was. As Frank stared at him, he swung an arm toward them, pointing something at them.

"Dive!" Frank knocked Joe down behind a row of seats before the person by the computer could fire. Only a loud click echoed in the auditorium—not gunfire.

The lights went out again.

"He's got a remote," Frank whispered, shaken. "He's wired the room."

"Great," Joe whispered back. "So we might

as well forget the lights. Is that what you're saying?"

"No, I'm saying we rush him," Frank replied.

"Is that a good idea? What if he has a gun?"

"What do you think?" Frank whispered.

Joe shrugged and leapt over the seat. Frank was right behind him. Together they charged the stage.

When they got there, the man who had been at the computer was gone.

"There!" Joe yelled, pointing toward the aisle on the far side of the auditorium. Through the darkness, Frank made out a figure in black with a small satchel.

"He's heading for the emergency exit!" Frank yelled. "Stop him!"

Before Frank finished speaking, Joe had leapt off the stage and was starting after the figure in black. The man was slowing down, probably winded by his run, but Joe took after him like a track star.

The man in black was too far ahead, though, and before Joe could reach him, the man made it through the emergency exit.

An alarm went off.

Frank ignored it. He went to the computer and gave it a quick examination as Joe took off after the man in black. Frank saw nothing noticeably wrong with the computer. As he moved away, something fluttered beside his boot. "A tissue," he said softly, remembering how Potrero had been blowing his nose earlier that evening. Of course the tissue could have been dropped there anytime. But it sure was close to the computer.

Frank put the tissue in his pocket and decided not to say anything about it until he'd had a chance to talk to Potrero.

Joe returned. "He got away, Frank. The exit opens on the parking lot. It's pretty dark back there. He could have blended in anywhere. You think it was Potrero?"

"I doubt it," Frank said. "Let's discuss it when we're out of here."

"Hold it right there!"

The lights came on. Frank spied a balding man in a camel-colored jacket standing next to the door, leaning over his unconscious partner. Over his breast pocket he wore a hotel security badge. He held a small walkie-talkie to his lips.

"Dillon here," Frank heard him say into the walkie-talkie. "I need some backup in the auditorium. And get Ms. Lassen down here, too. Now."

He snapped down the antenna and slid the walkie-talkie into his coat pocket. To Frank and Joe he said, "You two aren't going anywhere."

"Let's go through it once again," Hirsch said, pacing back and forth in front of them.

Frank and Joe sat on folding chairs in a drab little room. There was a ventilation duct over the door, but the room remained uncomfortably warm. The rest of the Camelot might have been medieval, but this employees' lounge was strictly twentieth century.

Hirsch wasn't the only one listening. Janet Lessen, half asleep and very upset, sat on a steel chair slightly behind the Hardys. The security guard, Dillon, was leaning against the back wall.

Frank retold his story for the third time, from his first encounter with the gamblers to the escape of the man from the auditorium. He had taken Hirsch aside earlier and promised to tell him about Joe's adventures later, when there were no other listeners. Hirsch was listening skeptically, pacing as if walking was the only way he could stay awake. Frank glimpsed the time on the clock on the wall.

It was four in the morning.

"So you see, I can't help you as far as the computer goes. Unless it has something to do with the two gamblers who took me for a ride. It's possible they wanted to fix the computer against me, but that doesn't make much sense since they think I'm still out in the desert. I think they work for Jerome Cornelius. Are you going to bring him in?"

"Nonsense," Hirsch growled, still pacing. "These clowns would never be so lucky as to work for a big shot like Cornelius. They're a couple of losers. They're only pretending to be connected to someone bigger, so they can scare you into doing what they want. Besides, there's nothing illegal about making bets in Las Vegas, and we have no proof that they tried to sabotage the computer.''

He stopped pacing and turned to Frank. "You're welcome to file charges against them for dumping you in the desert, though." Then he sighed. "I believe you're telling the truth, Frank. I want you to know that. Ms. Lassen, your turn.''

She twitched uncomfortably in her chair, then spoke up angrily. "Well, this is a difficult situation," she said. "The competition rules are very clear in saying that any contestant found in the playing room after hours faces immediate disqualification. However, since Sergeant Hirsch has accepted Mr. Hardy's story, and since no damage was done to the computer, I see no reason to remove Mr. Hardy from the tournament.''

"Thank you," Frank said.

"Don't thank me," she replied, standing. "I'm still very upset about this whole thing. But I think you know that this chess program represents several years' work by myself and others.''

She stopped herself and took a deep breath. "You will have to be penalized one game, Frank. I'm sorry, but that seems only fair.''

"What does that mean?" Joe said.

"That means I have to win all my games today," Frank replied, "and hope no one else gets more than five wins. The most I can get now is five—it would be six, but I lost that one game.''

"That's correct," Ms. Lassen said, grudgingly adding, "Good luck to you." She hurried out of the room.

The instant she left, Hirsch dismissed the security guard and turned to the Hardys. "All right," he said, keeping his back to the closed door. "What's this about Joe's day? Make it quick. I'm ready to hit the sack."

Briefly Joe told the sergeant about his near-drowning in the submerged car at Lake Mead, his discovery of Beth plotting with her kidnapper, whose name was Burke, and with a younger man who, they guessed, was her fiancé. He stopped short of suggesting that the fiancé might be involved in the chess tournament, though. They had no proof of that yet, as Frank had pointed out. The arrival of police on the scene might make it more difficult to find out what was going on.

"Good work, boys," Hirsch said when Joe had finished. "I have to say that I suspected something fishy was going on, what with that bank account and all." He hesitated, and Joe wondered whether he was deciding whether to believe them. "I'll get my people right on this," Hirsch said to Joe. "And now, if no one's got anything to add, I think we'll call it a night." He shot a look at Frank and Joe. "Don't do anything I wouldn't do. I mean that."

By the time the boys reached the twenty-second floor of the hotel, Frank noticed that Joe already had his key out. Fatigue washed over Frank, and now, half in the grip of sleep, he staggered toward their room, not certain he'd make it.

"Think it was Potrero?" he heard Joe ask behind him.

Frank blinked, fingering the tissue in his pocket. "Tampering with the computer? Why would he want to? If Potrero is the kidnapper, he wants the money; he doesn't want to mess up the game. I'm beginning to think it was someone paid by Iggy and Mose."

Joe shook his head. "Not likely. As far as they're concerned, you're out in the middle of the desert. You no longer pose a threat to them. And from what you've told me, Sergeant Hirsch is probably right. Between them they don't have the brains to brush their teeth, let alone rig a computer."

"They're smart enough to hire someone, though. And even with me out of the picture, they might have wanted to rig the odds on some other player."

"I'm too tired to think about it," Joe admitted as he opened the door to their room. "Let's forget about the computer for now. Tomorrow we can do background checks on all the male contestants. I want to find out for sure who's behind the kidnapping."

"Best idea I've heard all night," Frank agreed, following him inside. A hotel room had never looked so good to him. "Now let me concentrate. I need to work out some chess moves in my sleep."

Frank woke at nine that morning. He had hoped to practice some on his computer, but he barely had time to shower, dress, and eat before the auditorium opened for the day.

He wanted to be down there with Joe well before that.

By eleven-thirty he and Joe were studying the area just outside the auditorium. Off the lobby there was an alcove lined with phone booths. Joe took a seat in the nearest booth, picked up the handset, and held the receiver hook down while pretending to talk into the mouthpiece.

Frank stood in the lobby just outside the alcove. He watched for the other players. Carlene, Kyle, and Louisa arrived together, stopping to greet Frank before they went into the auditorium. When Mike passed by, he put a thumb to his nose and wiggled his fingers at Frank.

Victor appeared. "Hey, man. What are you standing here for? The game's inside."

"I'm waiting for someone," Frank said. He caught sight of George Potrero walking toward them. George looked as tired as Frank felt. He was clutching a wadded-up tissue in his hand.

"George!" Frank called out as George passed

them. The contestant walked by, paying no attention. Losing patience, Frank reached out and grabbed his shoulder. George stopped and stared at him in shock.

"I just wanted to say good luck, George," Frank said as Victor watched, bemused.

George gave Frank a confused half-smile, but said nothing. Mike stuck his head out of the auditorium and said sarcastically, "Need some help here?"

"I was just wishing George luck," Frank said. "It seems he still doesn't want to talk."

"Allow me," Mike said. He stepped in front of George and made a series of gestures with his hands. George gave a silent chuckle and clapped Frank on the shoulder. Mike and George went into the auditorium. Mike grinned back over his shoulder at Frank and waved.

Potrero is deaf, Frank realized. No wonder he never spoke to us. Mike talked to him in sign language. Did George even know his phone was ringing last night?

Frank felt like an idiot.

"You're a strange dude, Hardy," Victor said, chuckling as though he enjoyed seeing Frank embarrassed. Frank flushed, remembering how friendly Victor had pretended to be the day before. "I'll see you inside," Victor added as he walked away.

After they had gone, Joe stepped out of the

phone booth. "That was the guy all right," he said excitedly.

Frank shook his head. "No. We were wrong. George Potrero can't speak or hear. He couldn't be the guy in the car."

Joe looked dumbfounded. "That's impossible. You were just talking to him. I heard you!"

"Who?" Frank said.

"That last guy you were talking to."

Frank stared at him incredulously. "Victor?"

"I guess," Joe said. "The one who said, 'I'll see you inside.' There's no doubt in my mind, Frank. That was him!"

Chapter

13

"HEY, STRANGER," Victor called out as Frank entered the auditorium. "It's about time you showed up."

Frank forced himself to give a small, friendly wave to Victor, who was beaming at him from behind his computer terminal. Frank nodded politely to Janet Lassen, who stood at the center of the stage. Ms. Lassen looked as if she hadn't slept well, Frank noted as the woman checked her watch and glared at him. He was sorry he was responsible for the scare over her computer program. He liked her and didn't want to cause her problems.

Well, you're not helping much by being late, he told himself as he made his way to his seat. The last day of the competition was scheduled to begin in two minutes. The spectator seating area was half full already. In seats directly above and behind Frank, Cornelius and Elroy sat. Cornelius nodded to him, just to let Frank know he was there. Frank also spotted Iggy and Mose seated close by. Sergeant Hirsch was right, Frank realized. Clearly, Mose and Iggy didn't even recognize Cornelius, though he was sitting just ten rows away.

Frank grinned at the two gamblers, who were staring at him in disbelief. He could just imagine what they were thinking.

After he spotted Joe slipping into the back row, Frank turned and faced his terminal. He could feel Victor's piercing eyes on him and wondered why he hadn't suspected the over-friendly player before.

Ms. Lassen visited all of the contestants, saying a few final words to each player. When she got to Frank she leaned close and whispered, "We won't have any more escapades, will we, Mr. Hardy?"

"I promise," he said, trying to sound reassuring. "Six hours of chess and I'm out of here." Ms. Lassen's brow furrowed skeptically, but she moved on.

"Scoring points with the teacher?" Victor said to Frank in a stage whisper.

Frank closed his eyes. It was funny how that good-natured joke was nothing but ugly-sounding to Frank now. Victor was two terminals over, on the other side of Mike. On Frank's other side, Carlene tossed her red hair and chuckled. Mike raised his head briefly and rolled his eyes.

"She just wanted to make sure my brother wasn't going to walk out today, like he did yesterday," Frank replied.

As Frank expected, Victor nearly choked in surprise. The dark-haired boy caught his breath and forced a smile back onto his face. "Your brother's here?" he said. "I didn't know you had a brother."

Yeah, right, thought Frank. To Victor he said, "He should be around here somewhere."

"You haven't seen him today?"

Frank shrugged. "Not today, no. He'll show up, I'm sure."

Victor relaxed. Frank wasn't sure if Victor was relieved that Joe was out of commission, or reassured that his own role as Beth's fiancé hadn't been given away. Anyway, relaxed was how Frank wanted him. Frank leaned back in his chair and listened to Ms. Lassen repeat her preliminary speech from the day before and wish them all luck. Then a buzzer sounded.

The final round of games had begun.

An hour later Frank had already won one game, but he had a feeling that something was wrong. Ms. Lassen's perfect program botched what Frank considered a ridiculously simple trap when he cornered its king with a queen and a knight. The computer should have spotted that coming—Frank certainly would have, if the positions had been reversed.

The second game was harder, demanding greater concentration, but Frank took that one, too, by getting the pawn to the last row and turning it into a queen, then using that to block the escape of the computer's king.

The computer was losing in very simple situations.

Such easy chess gave Frank plenty of time to think about other things, and he now had a new candidate for the figure in black. It didn't look as if Iggy and Mose had hired anyone after all to alter the computer program, since Frank knew they wanted him to lose. But it was looking more and more as if whoever fiddled with the machine did affect the software after all. Frank knew the program's style pretty well by now, and the computer had never played so badly.

Frank considered calling Ms. Lassen over and telling her of his suspicions. But he decided not to. He needed to watch Victor, and after last night's episode Ms. Lassen would insist on Frank's presence at a full inquiry, leaving Victor free to move. Joe could follow Victor, of course, but there were too many people in the deadly game they were playing, and Frank knew he and Joe had to stick together or they'd continue to be sitting ducks.

Frank scanned the large overhead monitors. No one else was playing with Frank's ease. Most of the players were still on their first game of the day, and no one was winning.

Even Victor was sweating. Frank watched as the Californian put a pawn in the way of the computer's queen. The computer took the pawn, which lined the queen up to take Victor's second bishop. The loss wasn't that serious. What astonished Frank was that he could see a series of five simple moves that Victor could have made to put the computer in check. Victor wasn't trying any of them.

Frank was puzzled. He had watched Victor when he had the chance during the first round of games, and he knew Victor was a brilliant chess player. Yet now Victor was making moves that even Joe would have known enough to avoid.

Victor seemed to be trying to lose.

Frank played his third game more slowly, taking it in thirty-six moves. He dragged the fourth game out for the remaining hour and a half, using the time to keep track of Victor's playing. The Californian kept the play going for hours on a single game, never moving to checkmate.

This is a child's version of chess, Frank thought. Filled with nonsensical maneuvers, Victor's strategy seemed geared toward prolonging the game as long as possible. What was Victor trying to do?

One by one the others lost their last games. Louisa and George had managed to win one game each. The others had lost all four.

Frank moved his bishop to black king four, sealing his final win of the day. A buzzer sounded, and Frank's overhead monitor flashed brightly.

All but four members of the audience gave Frank a standing ovation. Iggy and Mose were sullen and angry. Cornelius and Elroy were utterly uninterested. Frank figured Cornelius had shown up just to keep an eye on him, hoping, perhaps, that Beth would magically materialize from backstage.

As the audience applauded, Ms. Lassen eyed Frank suspiciously. Frank watched her enter into a discussion with two other judges of the contest. Frank couldn't hear what they were saying, but he wasn't surprised when Ms. Lassen came to the microphone.

"I want to thank everyone for supporting the tournament. Because of unfortunate circumstances beyond our control, the award ceremony will be postponed until tomorrow."

She shot an aggrieved look at Frank as she and the other judges left without another word. Mike Ayres muttered something under his breath and walked off the stage in silence. The other competitors gathered around Frank to congratulate him.

Victor was the first to shake Frank's hand. "Congratulations, man. It couldn't happen to a nicer guy."

"I'd have thought you'd be more upset about losing," Frank said.

Victor laughed. "Easy come, easy go. Hey—thanks for everything."

Victor started off, and Frank shook hands with the other players, who were all eager to exchange addresses and discuss plans for a reunion. By the time Frank left the auditorium, Iggy and Mose had appeared near the exit, their hands inside their jacket pockets like movie gangsters. Frank hoped that Joe had followed Victor.

"We need to have a talk," Iggy said, so seriously that Frank almost laughed.

"You're right. Why don't we do that?" said a voice at the door. Iggy turned to find himself facing Sergeant Hirsch and two uniformed police officers. "Get them out of here," Hirsch snapped.

Slowly Iggy and Mose drew their empty hands from their pockets and raised them. The officers herded the gamblers away.

"Good work," Hirsch told Frank, nodding at the overhead monitor. "At least someone won something."

Cornelius approached. He was livid. "There

you are, Sergeant. I've been trying to reach you. I haven't heard a word from you or anyone else about my daughter in almost twenty-four hours. What do I have to do to get some action against a kidnapper in this town?"

"I was on my way up to talk to you, sir," Hirsch replied. "We have reason to believe your daughter is not in terrible danger. And we're closing in on the people responsible for her disappearance."

Cornelius turned even redder. "And you didn't tell me before? Give me their names, Hirsch. I'll take care of them myself. And it *won't* cost me a million dollars."

"You're absolutely right," Hirsch said, surprising both Frank and the middle-aged gangster. "We should have gotten a call from the kidnappers today, telling us what to do with the money. So far, there's been no call. You may as well take your money back, sir."

Hirsch glanced over Cornelius's shoulder and snapped his fingers. Another officer brought Joe over to join them. Frank felt deflated. So much for keeping tabs on Victor Julian.

"Boys, how would you like to help us get that money out of the bank?" Hirsch was saying. "It's a little after hours, but I've arranged for the manager to keep the bank open a while longer, just for us."

There was no way the Hardys could duck out of this responsibility. Flanked by police officers, they reluctantly accompanied Hirsch, Cornelius, and Elroy across the hotel lobby and into the bank. Frank scanned the lobby for a glimpse of Victor, but failed to spot the Californian. Cornelius came through loud and clear, though, when he whispered on the way, "I still hold you responsible for this, you little wise guy."

"Evening, Mr. Cornelius, Sergeant Hirsch," the manager said glumly as he locked the bank doors behind the group. They all gathered around the manager's desk as the heavyset older man shuffled through some papers and spread them across his desk with a look of desolation.

Poor guy, Frank thought. A man whose business is money must hate to see a million dollars leave his hands.

Hirsch produced the passbook for the savings account. "Anywhere special you want the money to go, Mr. Cornelius?"

"Certainly. To my personal account," Cornelius snapped. He produced a bank card and handed it to the bank manager. "Call the number on the back. They accept wire transfers anytime."

"Of course, sir." The manager gave Joe and Frank the transfer papers to sign, then gathered everything and rushed into the back. To Frank's surprise the man returned moments later, huffing

121

and puffing. He tried to speak, but it took him a moment to catch his breath.

It wasn't the hurrying that had colored the man's face beet red, Frank realized as the bank manager spoke. It was sheer terror.

"The money!" the man blubbered, panic-stricken. "Someone's emptied the account. Your million dollars is gone!"

Chapter

14

"WHAT?" Joe shouted, echoed loudly by Frank, Cornelius, and Hirsch.

"I checked," said the manager. "The money was withdrawn an hour ago by electronic transfer."

"How could that be?" Cornelius demanded. "No one has a bank card to that account. There'd be nothing to insert into a teller machine. Anyway, it's impossible to withdraw a million dollars that way."

The manager shook his head. "I know, I know. But the money is gone. We may be able to trace it, but not until business hours tomorrow."

"By which time it may be in some account in the Cayman Islands or Southeast Asia that we couldn't get to even if we could find it,'' Hirsch said.

"Arrest them!'' Cornelius shouted, enraged, pointing at the Hardys.

Joe ignored him. He was busy watching Frank. He could tell that Frank was thinking hard, working something out.

"On what charge?'' Hirsch asked Cornelius, annoyance starting to sound in his voice.

"Grand theft! Wire fraud! Kidnapping!'' Cornelius shouted, out of control. "I can't believe this. First my daughter disappears, and now my money!''

To Joe's relief, Hirsch met Cornelius's gaze calmly. "Listen,'' he said in a voice so soft it could barely be heard.

Conelius shut his mouth and swallowed hard, not missing the threat in Hirsch's whisper.

"It couldn't have been the Hardys,'' Hirsch continued. "I had the bankbook. These boys didn't even know the account number. They also didn't have a bank card or the identification number that goes with one. Without any of that, there's no remote access. The boys didn't steal your money.''

Joe tried to look innocent, even though he knew Frank had memorized the number. But Frank wouldn't have moved the money. Joe wondered suddenly if Victor had taken the million dollars.

"If that's all," Joe heard Frank say, "my brother and I would like to get going."

Hirsch shot him an odd look. "What's your hurry?"

Frank sighed. "We've signed all the papers we need to, right? It's been a long day, I'm tired, and I'd like to get some dinner and then rest for a while. If that's okay."

Hirsch nodded gravely. "Be my guests."

"You're going to let them go?" Cornelius shouted in outrage.

"Mr. Cornelius," Hirsch said, "please." To the Hardys he said, "Boys, enjoy yourselves in Las Vegas. Thank you for your cooperation."

As the Hardys reached the door, Hirsch added cryptically, "Good game. I guess we're in checkmate."

"Winning already?" said Frank with a grin. By the way he said it, Joe knew they still had a gambit left to play.

"Okay, so tell me. What's next?" Joe demanded as soon as they were out of the bank. He had to break nearly into a run to keep up with Frank. Joe glanced back over his shoulder to see Cornelius still inside the bank, arguing with Hirsch, and he figured his brother had been smart to leave. Joe didn't want to be around when Cornelius and Elroy started after them. He had the feeling that if Cornelius couldn't get his money back, he wouldn't mind balancing the books with their lives.

Frank slowed down as they neared the banks of slot machines, where they could mingle with the crowd and avoid being seen. Frank narrowed his eyes, scanning the crowd as he stalked the rows of one-armed bandits.

"Look for Victor," he told Joe.

"Okay," Joe said, surprised. "But I doubt he's here. If he took the money, he could be on his way to the Caribbean by now."

Joe hadn't had a good look at the slots since they arrived in the Camelot. That day it seemed as though twice as many people were playing them. He noticed that no one had yet won the grand prize of a million dollars. For a fleeting moment he wished he were old enough to win the money and use it to get Cornelius off their backs. But he knew the odds against winning were ridiculously high. People who gambled because they needed the money usually ended up in a much worse situation.

Dutifully Joe followed his brother to a section of the lobby that overlooked the shallow pit full of slot machines but wasn't on the playing floor, so the security guards wouldn't try to apprehend them for gambling underage. From there, Joe noticed, they could also keep an eye on everyone entering and leaving the elevators. "I don't see any sign of Victor," Joe said.

"I just hope he hasn't left town already," Frank muttered.

"We could check the airlines," said Joe. He wished he'd gone ahead and checked the contestants' backgrounds that morning, but he hadn't had time, and anyway, he hadn't felt he needed to after identifying Victor's voice. If he knew more about the boy, he realized now, he might have a better idea of what to do next.

"Frank," Joe said cautiously, "you knew our bank account number. You didn't somehow take the million, did you?"

Frank laughed. "Not a chance, Joe. Victor did, and I know how."

"Impossible," said Joe. "The manager said the money was taken an hour ago while Victor was with you, playing chess in the auditorium. I saw him."

"That's when he got it," Frank explained. "Remember, last night they couldn't find any tampering with the computer or their program? They weren't looking for the right thing. Victor wasn't after the computer or the program. He was after the cables going to the computer."

"So that was Victor in the auditorium last night," Joe said. "When did you figure that out?"

"Mostly during the tournament, but I wasn't absolutely sure until we got the news about the money being stolen. Victor comes from Silicon

Valley, one of the biggest centers of computer research in the country."

"Think he knows as much about computers as you do?"

"A lot more, if he can pull this off," Frank said. "When Victor was in the auditorium last night, he was hooking up the computer to the cables running under the floor. I bet if we checked we'd find that all the hotel's computer cables run through there, including the cable to the bank."

"So he hooked up the computer to the bank cable," Joe said. "So what?"

"So all computer programs are essentially alike. It doesn't matter if it's a chess game or a bank code. Basically it takes the same kind of basic programming, which consists of answering a million questions yes or no until the computer does exactly what you want it to.

"I saw Victor making a lot of bizarre moves that seemed to have no point. Joe, those weren't chess moves. Victor was using the chess game to input data into the computer system."

Joe was puzzled. "I don't know that much about computers, but wouldn't he need software to do that? They said there wasn't anything wrong with their software."

Frank frowned. "I haven't figured that part out yet. But he did use software, and his program corrupted the chess software. No program, no matter how good, is perfect. He corrupted the computer program enough to give me easy games, something it wasn't supposed to do. That's how I won.''

''But I still don't see how he got the money.''

Frank grinned in grudging appreciation of Victor's know-how. ''His chess moves were translated into banking codes. Victor just told the bank what account to access and what to do with the money. Joe, he used the chess game to rob the bank, and nobody even knew it! It was brilliant!''

Joe nodded. Then his face lit up. ''Here's your chance to tell him,'' he told his brother.

Joe pointed to one of the elevators just as Victor stepped out, smiling. He had changed into a loud Hawaiian shirt and was leisurely strolling through the lobby. Obviously, Joe realized, he didn't know anyone suspected him of a crime.

''Joe, we've got to get out of sight!'' said Frank. He leapt off the raised floor into the gaming area. Joe joined him without asking why. He didn't want to be seen, either.

Joe had more in mind than nabbing Victor and getting the money back. They still had to find Beth, and he had a few lumps to give back to Burke as well.

Victor walked by without seeing them. Joe saw that despite his casual air, the Californian was jingling the change in his pockets nervously. Perhaps he wasn't so sure he'd gotten away with a major theft after all.

"Hey, boys!" Joe heard a gruff voice behind him. He and Frank turned to find themselves facing a mean-looking security guard. "No underage guests are allowed in the gaming room. I can throw you out of this hotel for that."

"Don't bother. We're going," said Joe. He pushed past the guard and bolted toward the exit. Frank was right behind him. The guard sputtered and yelled, but Joe didn't have time to listen. They had to catch up to Victor, who was leaving the hotel.

"There he is!" Joe yelled as they pushed their way outside. He had spotted Victor in the parking lot, ducking into a blue car.

Frank dashed to the taxi stand and got into the first cab in line. The driver started the engine, and Joe leapt in after Frank.

"Where to?" the cabbie said.

"Ever done a tail job?" asked Frank.

"Like on TV?" the cabbie asked, astounded. "Nah, but it sounds like fun. Let's go for it."

"Finally," Joe said when the blue car pulled into a parking lot as the sun was setting. Victor got out of his car and locked it. The cab pulled up to the lot, and Frank paid the driver with the last of his money. "For a minute I thought he was going to drive home to California."

"The Hoover Dam, huh?" the cabbie said. "You should have said you were tourists. I would have given you a special rate."

The cab left, and Joe looked up at the gigantic Hoover Dam. Built in 1936, the structure was over seven hundred feet tall. It held back the mighty Colorado River on one side and forced its waters into Lake Mead. The huge dam with its breathtaking views was a popular tourist attraction, but Joe knew that that night it would be the site of the end of a criminal career.

They followed Victor on foot at a distance. He never looked back, and as far as Joe could tell, the Californian had no idea he was being followed. Frank and Joe hung back as Victor walked out onto the dam's observation deck—an area dwarfed by the sweep of the dam itself. It was late in the day so there were very few people around.

"Look," Joe said, nudging his brother. "There's Beth—and that must be Burke."

"It looks like something's wrong," said Frank.

Joe nodded. He could see that Beth's eyes were downcast. Victor appeared nervous as he approached Burke slowly.

Then under the lights, which had just come on, Joe spotted the gun in Burke's hand.

"The hired gun takes over," Frank said.

They watched Burke gesture with his gun at Victor. Victor nodded and reached into his shirt pocket. He brought out a small card that flashed silver in the light as he continued talking.

"That's a bank card," Frank guessed. "How

much do you want to bet it gives the bearer access to a million bucks?''

Even from that distance, Joe could see that there was a disagreement between the two men over something. Burke was gesturing angrily with his gun while Victor held the card out of reach and tried to grab Beth out of Burke's grasp.

"I guess he's trying to trade the million dollars for Beth," Frank said. "Interesting. Beth gets kidnapped after all."

"Yeah, very interesting," Joe said, already moving forward. "Let's go."

"Okay, both of you," Joe yelled as he and Frank jogged onto the observation deck toward the trio. "Give it up now. It's all over, anyway. We're on to you."

Burke's eyes flashed at Victor. "Double-crossing—"

Before Victor could move, Burke shoved Beth at the safety railing. She was bent backward over it, screaming. As Joe lunged to save her, Burke reached down, grabbed her ankle, and lifted her up, forcing her almost all the way over. Joe caught sight of pounding water seven hundred feet below.

He charged Burke and grabbed Beth's other leg and pulled her back onto the pavement. Joe then sprang to his feet, ready to deal with Burke.

Frank was already on the kidnapper and was wrestling with him against the railing.

Joe and Victor stared in horror as Frank and Burke pushed each other farther and farther over the railing. Grunting, each tried to gain an advantage against the strip of metal.

"Frank! Move back!" Joe shouted, starting toward him. He was too late to help. As Joe watched, Frank slowly slid over the railing. In an instant he would plunge to his death in the raging waters below!

Chapter

15

"No!" Frank thrust his arm up and grabbed for the railing, folding one hand around it just in time. Burke stood poised, ready to uncoil Frank's fingers and drop him into the water below. It was a losing battle for Frank until Victor rammed his head into Burke, knocking him out of the way.

"There," Victor grunted. He locked his fingers around Frank's wrist and pulled on him, anchoring himself with his other hand on the railing. "Now climb up."

His pulse racing, Frank started up. Just then Burke got back up and lunged at Victor.

"Joe!" Frank yelled desperately. "Get over here!"

"I'm here!" he heard Joe say as Burke knocked

Victor over the railing, kicking Frank's anchor hand loose. Victor managed to grab the railing as Frank, plunging, reached out and desperately wrapped his arms around Victor's legs. Both boys were now being supported by Victor's one hand. Joe tackled Burke and had him down and out in short order.

"Get over here, Beth!" Frank screamed. "Without your help we're going to fall!"

Beth went into action and grabbed for Victor's belt. Together she and Joe began to pull him and Frank to safety.

Joe hoped Frank had enough strength left to hold on to Victor.

"You're doing it, Joe," Frank gasped, his eyes popping up over the edge of the ledge. "Just a little more—"

Frank's knuckles brushed the railing, which he managed to grip. "Let's go," he told Joe.

Frank finally pulled himself up and over the railing. "Look out!" he heard Joe shout. He turned to see Burke kneeling and holding a .45.

"You're all dead," Burke muttered under his breath, his gun hand braced against his knee.

Joe whirled around and lashed out with his foot, catching Burke in the wrist. The burly man dropped his hand to the concrete, and Joe stomped his foot down, smacking the gun barrel into the pavement. Burke's wrist twisted sideways, and he shrieked in pain as he pulled the trigger.

A shot exploded across the concrete, causing the few remaining tourists to scream and scatter. Then, to Frank's relief, Joe kicked the gun away.

Crazed with rage, Burke stood up and charged at Frank. At the last second Frank ducked and Burke went sailing over the railing. With a blood-curdling scream, Burke dropped, a blurred shadow against the dark frothy water. Then he was gone.

"Oh, no," Beth moaned as she stared in silence at the empty space where Burke had been.

Frank pulled himself over the railing and lay panting on the concrete.

Frank vaguely noticed that even Victor, usually so talkative and friendly, was shocked into silence by what had just occurred.

Joe and Victor helped Frank sit up on the concrete while the handful of late tourists backed away, frightened.

"It's all over for you guys," Joe muttered angrily to Victor and Beth while they all waited for Frank to recover from the shock of what had happened.

Frank watched the couple, sitting on the observation deck with their arms around each other.

"You mean you're not going to let us go?" Victor asked, astonished.

Joe stared at his brother in amazement.

136

Neither Hardy could believe he had heard the question. "Why would we let you go?" Joe demanded. "After all the trouble you've put us through—"

"You don't understand," Victor said.

Joe was about to tell Victor off when Frank raised a hand, signaling Joe to be quiet. "Let's hear it," Frank told Victor.

"I met Beth two years ago," Victor began, putting all his earnestness into his voice. "There was a careers seminar for high school students in Dallas. Both of us attended. I was a senior; she was a junior. We saw each other one day and that was that. I couldn't stop thinking about her. I didn't know she couldn't stop thinking about me, either."

"We exchanged addresses and phone numbers at the end of the seminar," Beth said. "We started writing and calling each other every week, and pretty soon we both knew how we felt. That was how my father found out. He discovered Victor's letters and read them. He ordered me not to write him back, and not to talk to him. He'd never met Victor, but he hated him. My father hates the very thought of Victor."

"He always calls you his little girl," Frank said. "He wants to protect you."

"Yeah?" said Victor. "Is that why he sent Elroy to threaten me? My doorbell rang one day, and when I answered it, Godzilla was standing there threatening to pound me into the ground if

I so much as thought about Beth again. I remember my little sister just standing there watching us and screaming. Of course I visited Beth in secret several times in New York after that, and the whole time I thought about how I was going to get Beth and pay Cornelius back."

"Wait a minute," Frank said. *"What* sister? I thought you said you were an only child and had no real family."

Victor reddened. "Okay, so I made up some stories. I was feeling kind of cocky, getting away with my plan. It felt good to be able to fool a guy as smart as you. So I sliced the baloney a little thick, I guess."

"So you figured you'd rob Beth's father," Joe interrupted.

"Do you know how he got his money?" Beth said, outraged. "He's a gangster—a common criminal."

"It wasn't enough to rob him," Victor said, remorse creeping into his voice. "We wanted him to be grief stricken, the way he made us feel. I started sending my letters to Beth through a friend of hers, and we stayed in touch that way. Then this chess tournament came up, and I started thinking . . ."

"Not very well, I'm afraid," Frank said. "What made you think you could pull it off?"

"We almost did, didn't we?" Victor replied. A flicker of his old reckless charm appeared in his handsome face. "We still can, if you'll help us."

Frank shook his head. "I can't do that. We figured out the rest of it, except for a couple of things. Ms. Lassen said they checked the chess software after you tampered with the computer, and they didn't find anything wrong. But you must have put in a software bomb in order to pull off that money-transfer scam. How on earth did you do that?"

Victor laughed. "My uncle was one of the programmers who wrote the code for the original version of that chess program. He's the one who got me interested in computers in the first place. When he got the assignment, he asked me if I wanted to work on it with him. And I did."

Now Frank understood. "So the chess program had the transfer capability all the time. Pretty neat. Now tell me—why did you get us involved?"

"Because of your reputation," Victor said, acting excited again. "Most people don't know about you, but people on computer bulletin boards swap gossip, and news gets around. Beth was coming from your area, and we needed a decoy. It was like you were sent for us, Frank," he said with a piercing gaze. "We never intended to hurt anyone. Beth and I just wanted to be together. We were going to take the money— which would have been Beth's anyway, some-day—give Burke his cut, and go somewhere

THE HARDY BOYS CASEFILES

where Cornelius would never find us. You've got to believe me."

"You never intended to hurt anyone?" Joe piped up. "Burke tried to drown me in a car in Lake Mead, Beth beat me with a radio, and then Burke tried to shoot me on the Strip—but you never intended to hurt anyone? Forget it, you two aren't going anywhere."

Beth was aghast. "Burke told us he dumped the car because the police were looking for it. I never knew anyone was in it. I thought you'd traced us to the cabin on purpose and were going to turn us in. I know I hit you too hard, but you scared me to death!" Beth's expression changed. "What do you mean, Burke tried to shoot you?"

"It doesn't matter," Frank said. "The fact is, both Burke and Cornelius—and a couple other guys you probably don't even know about— could have killed us any number of times. And it's all your fault. I agree with Joe. We have to turn you in."

"Frank," Victor pleaded. "Please listen. I didn't know what kind of man Burke was. I just knew he was a private detective here in Vegas, and he understood computers and security systems. I went to him for help in setting up the shielded bank account to put the money into. He found out what we were doing and cut himself in for a piece of the action. I didn't know he was a killer, and I didn't know he was planning to take all the money. He would have taken everything if you hadn't shown up."

"I guess that's one you owe us," Joe said. "Let's go."

"Please!" Victor said. "If you take us in, they'll send us both to prison."

"Funny thing, buddy boy," said an unexpected voice. "That's exactly what I had in mind."

The four of them turned to face Jerome Cornelius. The slight, bespectacled man's sharklike smile was gone, replaced by a hurt and angry scowl. In his hand was a pistol—the mate of the one in Elroy's hand.

"Cornelius!" Joe said. "How—"

"Easy. We followed you in that cab." Cornelius scrunched up his face and looked Victor over. "This is the type you go for, Beth? I thought you had better taste." He glanced at his henchman. "Get Beth to the car while I remove these spots from the face of the earth."

"Don't!" Beth ordered. Before anyone could stop her, she scooped up the gun Joe had kicked out of Burke's hand. Beth held it leveled at Cornelius.

"If you hurt Victor, I'll kill you," she said, her voice shaking.

"Put that down, Beth," Joe said, edging toward her. "You don't want to shoot your father."

"He's right," Cornelius told Beth. "You're

upset. I understand that. Put the gun down and everything will be okay.''

Beth's mouth turned down in anger and hatred. Slowly she squeezed the trigger. Joe hurled himself against her, fighting her for control of Burke's revolver.

Frank flinched as a shot rang out and someone screamed.

Chapter

16

JOE GRABBED THE GUN away from Beth and pushed her down to get her out of the line of fire. He spun toward the source of the shot.

"Put it down!" Joe heard someone call. He turned to see Sergeant Hirsch silhouetted against the pink and deep purple sky, gripping a service revolver in both hands. He had it aimed at Cornelius, who was nursing his shoulder. Two uniformed officers stood ready to aid the sergeant. A good distance behind them a growing number of tourists watched in fascination and horror.

"No problem, sir," Joe put up both his hands, dangling the gun on one finger by the trigger guard. Slowly he crouched, his arms spread wide, and set the gun on the concrete.

"Nice of you to show up, Sergeant," Frank said from behind Joe.

"You don't think Cornelius is the only person capable of tailing someone, do you?" Hirsch said. "I had a man on him from the second he left the bank. Looks like we can all go downtown and sort this out."

"Sergeant," Cornelius protested, "I was just protecting my daughter."

"Around here we call that kind of protection attempted murder," Hirsch said. "You're going to be spending more time in our state than you'd planned this trip, Mr. Cornelius. In fact, I think you ought to know you have the right to remain silent. . . ."

He turned to Victor a while later. "As for you—assuming we drop the charge of kidnapping, since the young lady here is eighteen and wasn't abducted against her will, you're still looking at charges of extortion, fraud, bank robbery, and computer sabotage—and those are just a few of the crimes that come to mind. It's up to the district attorney to decide if she'll prosecute. But if I get any trouble out of you I'll break you into tiny little pieces. Got it?"

"Got it," Victor said glumly.

Hirsch extended an arm toward two squad cars. "Ladies and gentlemen, if you please."

Resigned and relieved, Joe started for the cruisers. Just then he saw a sudden blur out of the corner of his left eye. He turned in time to see Elroy smash both fists backward, catching both police officers assigned to guard him in the face and knocking them right off their feet. Hirsch spun toward him, and Elroy's fist connected, knocking the sergeant out.

"Watch out!" Joe yelled as Cornelius scooped up Hirsch's gun and fired at Victor as the boy sprinted away. The shot was wild, going over Victor's head. Before Joe could move, Frank tackled Victor, knocking him to the ground out of the line of fire.

Joe spun around again in time to see Cornelius lunge for his daughter. Joe stepped in the man's way, and Cornelius's pistol cracked across his head, stunning him.

"Stop them," Joe mumbled through a haze of pain, as he watched Cornelius grab Beth's hand and push her toward Elroy. The enormous man picked her up and threw her over his shoulder.

The trio reached Cornelius's luxury car before Joe, Frank, or Victor could react. As the red import sped away, Joe saw Victor push Frank aside and spring to his feet. Joe started to race after the boy, but the pain of the blow from the gun sent him back onto his knees.

"Are you okay?" Frank said, gently shaking his brother.

"I think so," Joe said, rubbing his eyes. He spied Victor running toward his blue car, and he gritted his teeth.

"Not this time," Joe said to himself.

Before Frank could stop him, Joe was back on his feet, sprinting awkwardly toward the blue car. Victor started the engine and hit the gas. As the blue car screeched across Joe's path, Joe jumped at it, catching hold of the open driver's window just in time. "Whoa!" Joe yelled as he pulled himself painfully up against the side of the car. He snaked his arm in through the window and wrapped it around Victor's neck.

"Stop this car," said Joe. "Now!"

"They're getting away!" Victor shouted in frustration as he put on the brakes. Joe motioned to Frank, who was using the police radio in Hirsch's car to call for help.

"So let's go get them," Joe said after Frank was inside with Victor and him.

Victor stared at him for a moment, dumbfounded. Then he threw the car into gear and raced back onto the road to Las Vegas.

"There they are!" Joe cried a short time later as Victor's car sped past the Las Vegas city limits and the brilliantly lit city flashed against the dark sky. Joe was relieved to have spotted the red import. It had stayed far ahead of them all the way back to las Vegas, impossible to tail in the dark, and Joe knew Victor was terrified that he might have lost Beth forever.

"What luck," Frank observed. The import was pulling into the spotlit valet parking area at the Camelot. Instead of fleeing town, Joe realized, Cornelius was going back to the hotel, probably to collect what was in his room. When he thought about it, Joe saw that his behavior fit what they knew about the man. Cornelius had a habit of living his life as though he were above the law.

"Maybe we can sneak up on them," Joe began, but then he saw the determined look in Victor's eye. Victor floored the gas, and the car leapt the curb and roared over the Camelot's lawn.

As they approached, Joe saw Elroy climb out of the import and walk around the front of it. Clearly Elroy didn't see Victor's car shooting across the lawn at thirty miles an hour.

"Jump!" Joe heard Frank yell. Instinctively the brothers knocked open their doors and threw themselves from the car, landing on the soft green grass.

As he landed, Joe heard the car smash into the side of the import. Joe sat up in time to see the red car leap forward, knocking Elroy over and causing several onlookers to scream. Then Joe saw the big man fall unconscious to the pavement.

Joe stared through the darkness as Victor, dazed but triumphant, staggered out of his dented car.

"Victor! Watch out!" Joe yelled as he saw Cornelius burst from the far side of the import, pulling Beth behind him with one hand and firing his gun with the other. Before Victor could react, a shot clipped him in the shoulder. He dropped to his knees in shock, holding his arm.

Seeing Victor drop, Beth screamed and slapped at her father. "I hate you!" Joe heard her scream. "All you ever do is hurt people! Why don't you leave us alone?"

From what Joe could tell, the savageness of her attack surprised Cornelius, and he loosened his grip. Beth broke free and ran to Victor.

Frank and Joe got to their feet and closed in on Cornelius.

"Stay away!" Cornelius said, taking shelter behind the red car and waving the gun. His eyes darted from the Hardys to the other faces staring at him. A crowd was slowly closing in. With a growl, Cornelius threw the pistol at Frank and broke away, heading for the hotel lobby.

"Come on, Frank," Joe said, breaking into a trot. They entered the hotel a moment later and stopped in disbelief. "He's gone," Joe said. But that didn't make sense. Cornelius hadn't had time to make it to the elevators, and only three people stood near the checkout desk. The man had disappeared.

"He must be in the gambling area," Frank decided, gazing over the banks and banks of slot machines. "There's nowhere else he could have gone."

"Oh, great. We'll never find him in there," Joe replied.

Frank only shrugged. Joe looked out over the slot-machine room, which was crowded with hundreds of people. He knew the security guard was somewhere in there, with his eyes peeled for them. Even if they somehow managed to elude him, Joe knew they had almost no chance of finding Cornelius. The man had escaped.

All at once Joe heard a chorus of bells and whistles, and small fireworks spit harmless sparks into the crowds below. A spotlight burned down on the slot machine area from the high ceiling, and the crowd parted to stare at the source of the excitement.

Next Joe spotted an excited little man with glasses clearing a path toward the spotlight.

"What's this?" Joe asked, watching the round man clear his throat into a wireless microphone.

But the little man was already speaking. "The Camelot Hotel wants to congratulate its latest top prize winner!" he cried as the bells and whistles subsided.

Joe stared as a neon sign flashed against the wall. " 'One million dollar winner,' " he read aloud. "Someone hit the jackpot!"

The crowd applauded wildly as the winner appeared to take a bow. Then Joe saw who it was and started to laugh. Frank began to laugh, too. To Joe's delight, Sergeant Hirsch pressed in through the door just then, shaking with anger—but in moments he was laughing, too.

To Joe it seemed the only one who was not

laughing was Cornelius, who stood in front of the slot machines and, with a sickly grimace, held up a giant fake check for one million dollars.

"To the winner of our tournament we present this check for ten thousand dollars," Ms. Lassen announced excitedly.

With the other contestants, Frank stood and applauded as George Potrero approached the lectern at the front of the filled auditorium. For the first time Frank saw a smile on George's face, and it made him feel good. In his way, he felt, he had made up for his suspicions about George by disqualifying himself as champion. It was an honor Frank could not accept, knowing how he had won. He looked around the audience, exchanging thumbs-up with the other contestants. Even Mike Ayres gave in and raised one thumb in agreement. Frank smiled. He was already looking forward to the reunion a year from now.

After the ceremony Frank got two plates of cake from the refreshment table and took one over to Joe. They sat down on the stage next to Victor and Beth. Victor was excitedly explaining the intricate workings of the chess program while Beth listened, looking a little bored.

"So what did the D.A. say?" Joe asked Victor before chomping down on a big bite of fluffy cake.

Victor stopped talking and drew a deep breath.

"She took all morning straightening things out with the feds, but it looks like I'll get off with giving the money back to Beth's dad and doing a lot of community service."

"Mr. Cornelius won't be spending much of that money where he's going for the next few years," Joe pointed out. "It was assaulting cops that put him over the top."

"Tell them the good part," Beth said to Victor.

Her fiancé smiled. "Community service means I'll have to spend my summers here in Las Vegas for the next few years to put in the hours. But that's okay, because the people at the bank decided that instead of pressing charges they're going to ask me to teach them how to keep other computer experts from breaking into their lines. Also, my community service will involve setting up a computer network system for gamblers' therapy workshops. I think I could get into doing good stuff like that."

His expression grew serious. "Listen, guys, I want to apologize for involving you two. I didn't think things would get so out of hand. Basically I guess I was trying to be a lot cleverer than I am. I learned my lesson, if that means anything to you."

"Don't worry about it," Frank said graciously. "By the way, I bet I could recommend a couple of customers for your gamblers' workshops."

"Oh, yeah?" Beth said, interested. "Who?"

Frank pointed at two men hunched down in seats at the far end of the auditorium, wolfing down cake.

"Iggy and Mose," Frank announced with mock solemnity. "They probably wish they'd never even heard about this chess tournament."

"What are you talking about?" Joe said. "Take a closer look at them. They bet *against* you in the end, remember?"

Frank blinked. Then he studied the pair of gamblers again. That was true—both men had huge grins plastered across their faces. As Frank and the others watched, a waiter came to offer the two men snacks from a tray. Iggy took a tiny sandwich and, with a big flourish, left a handful of bills in its place.

"What'd I tell you?" Joe reminded Frank. "Fun City, U.S.A. Now, how about getting out of here and having a *real* good time!"

Frank and Joe's next case:

Will wonders never cease? Chet Morton, the original couch potato, has joined Bayport's new state-of-the-art health club. But the Hardys know what's *really* on his mind, and her name is Dawn Reynolds, aerobics instructor. One mystery solved, an even bigger one awaits: The boys have found that working out in the club's weight-training room may be hazardous to their health.

Chet ends up in the hospital, and another of the club's members ends up in the bay . . . dead! Frank and Joe suspect that an underworld gang has muscled in on the action. The Hardys know they're in for the fight of their lives, because when push comes to shove, these are the kind of thugs who'll stop pumping iron and start spraying lead . . . in *Cold Sweat,* Case #63 in the Hardy Boys Casefiles.℠

Most Archway Paperbacks are available at special quantity discounts for bulk purchases for sales promotions, premiums or fund raising. Special books or book excerpts can also be created to fit specific needs.

For details write the office of the Vice President of Special Markets, Pocket Books, 1230 Avenue of the Americas, New York, New York 10020.

SUPER HIGH TECH ... SUPER HIGH SPEED ... SUPER HIGH STAKES!

TOM SWIFT®

VICTOR APPLETON

He's daring, he's resourceful, he's cool under fire. He's Tom Swift, the brilliant teen inventor racing toward the cutting edge of high-tech adventure.

Tom has his own lab, his own robots, his own high-tech playground at Swift Enterprises, a fabulous research lab in California where every new invention is an invitation to excitement and danger.

- ☐ **TOM SWIFT 1 THE BLACK DRAGON** ....67823-X/$2.95
- ☐ **TOM SWIFT 2 THE NEGATIVE ZONE** ....67824-8/$2.95
- ☐ **TOM SWIFT 3 CYBORG KICKBOXER** ....67825-6/$2.95
- ☐ **TOM SWIFT 4 THE DNA DISASTER** ....67826-4/$2.95
- ☐ **TOM SWIFT 5 MONSTER MACHINE** ....67827-2/$2.99
- ☐ **TOM SWIFT 6 AQUATECH WARRIORS** ....67828-0/$2.99
- ☐ **TOM SWIFT 7 MOONSTALKER** ....75645-1/$2.99
- ☐ **TOM SWIFT 8 THE MICROBOTS** ....75651-6/$2.99

Simon & Schuster Mail Order Dept. VAA
200 Old Tappan Rd., Old Tappan, N.J. 07675

Please send me the books I have checked above. I am enclosing $_____ (please add 75¢ to cover postage and handling for each order. Please add appropriate local sales tax). Send check or money order–no cash or C.O.D.'s please. Allow up to six weeks for delivery. For purchases over $10.00 you may use VISA: card number, expiration date and customer signature must be included.

Name _____

Address _____

City _____ State/Zip _____

VISA Card No. _____ Exp. Date _____

Signature _____ 246-07